The Wizard's Mistake

Tales of Halziyon, Book 1

Daniel P. Riley

The Wizard's Mistake
Tales of Halziyon, Book 1

Copyright © 2023 by Daniel P. Riley

Paperback ISBN: 978-1-63812-658-4
Ebook ISBN: 978-1-63812-659-1

All rights reserved. No part in this book may be produced and transmitted in any form or by any means, electronic, or mechanical, including photocopying, recording, or by any information storage and retrieval system, without permission in writing from the copyright owner.

The views expressed in this work are solely those of the author and do not necessarily reflect the views of the publisher. It hereby disclaims any responsibility for them.

Published by Pen Culture Solutions   03/21/2023

Pen Culture Solutions
1-888-727-7204 (USA)
1-800-950-458 (Australia)
support@penculturesolutions.com

Dedication

To everyone who isn't sure they're good enough.

And to my mother for always telling me I was better than I believed.

THE WIZARD'S MISTAKE

Written by Daniel P. Riley

Cover art by Ariana Riley

Chapter One:
Is this really necessary?

Yoder Hals wasn't well-liked in his hometown. His father had been a great man who passed when he was only seven years old. Yoder had grown up under the tender, loving care of his mother: Doreen. Doreen doted on her only son all the way up to now, his seventeenth turn of the seasons. This made Yoder, according to the villagers, a spoiled, fat little jerk.

The truth was that Yoder Hals was an overweight young man with short, sandy blonde hair and gentle blue eyes. He simply lacked any confidence. What the villagers of Mater's Range in the sprawling countryside of Halziyon thought was arrogance was, in fact, a crippling fear of everything. Yoder had no one to teach him to brawl or drink or farm or even shave his face. So, his mother did it for him once he began to sprout the first scruff of puberty on his round chin and jowls last cycle.

She even chose his clothing for him, dressing the chubby lad in wine red or berry blue like his father. He even wore his father's old belt and boots, which Doreen lovingly repaired over and over again. The leathers were marred in crisscrossing stitchwork that seemed almost fashionable.

In fact, Yoder could have learned from any of the other men in Mater's Range had he not been so afraid of failing. He hid from them altogether in the open fields surrounding the sleepy little hamlet. Mater's Range was named for its founder, Mater Molovi, some fifty cycles passed. While the quiet, comfortable town with its quiet comfortable houses with their thatched roofs and quiet, comfortable hearths billowed smoke into the sky, the men tended fields and livestock, or fished and turned to crafting while the women laundered and gathered and cooked in quiet, comfortable peace. It was all really quiet and really comfortable.... until one bright, sunny morning.

Before that bright, sunny morning, there was a dark and silent evening. It preceded a long and gentle night-time as these things tend to go. Yoder Hals sat down at the plain wooden table in the common room of his little house where he and his mother lived their quiet, comfortable lives. Upon the table was a spread of sliced and salted ham, mashed potatoes (which were his favorites), a bowl of boiled beans, and a nice, wildberry pie. Yoder licked his lips eagerly as he began to pile generous helpings of each onto his plate. All except for the pie; that would be for after. Two slices of Ham, a heaping spoonful of potatoes and beans filled his plate. Doreen poured a tankard of sweet wine. She'd traded a pie for the wine with Narys next door and brought it to sit before him.

"Here you go, my love. A nice drink to wash it all down with. Eat up, poppet." she said, ruffling Yoder's clean, trimmed sandy hair with her worn fingers. Doreen worked hard all day, washing and gathering, and baking to trade with her neighbors. All so she could provide anything her son would ever need. Yoder ran about the fields, daydreaming about adventures he'll never have the courage to face. Slaying dragons and rescuing fair maidens who will do all manner of lewd things in gratitude.

"Thank you, Mum," Yoder replied, slicing a bite of ham to shove into his mouth a mere moment afterward. He devoured his dinner in relative silence. Doreen regaled him with the tales of her day, baking pies and loaves of bread for the neighbors.

She gossiped about Narys' mother's rickety cough or Hanstel's courtship of Ola Yorg's daughter Eliza, who had a queer eye that made her appear to be looking in two directions at once. Yoder tuned her out by then, relishing in his feast. He soon announced he was going to bed and left her behind to clean up whilst he trotted off to his room.

Where Doreen slept in a cot by the hearth below in the common room, Yoder was given the loft. According to his mother; a young man needs his own space. The loft had been where she and Yoder's father slept before he passed away but soon after, it was given to the boy. Yoder climbed the ladder with great effort.

He paused at the top to catch his breath before he stumbled three steps on the rug-covered wood. One foot kicked off a boot, then helped the other free. Both were left there as he padded over to the window and lit the little candle in its little bronze base.

The yellow light flickered, illuminating a straw bed covered in linens that desperately needed a wash. A pile of blankets was shoved against the far wall where the bed lay. He had pushed it aside when he woke, then wandered off without bothering to flatten them out. A wooden chest of drawers was set beside the bed. They hung open with garments stuffed here and there haphazardly. A faint buzzing sound became clear. Yoder frowned at the noise before pattering about to locate the source.

Under the bed was a trunk left by his late father. Beside it lay his father's heirloom sword in its wooden scabbard. Next to that was a plate with the rotted, festering meat and bone of a bird gathering flies. Yoder huffed, annoyed by its presence.

He picked it up and then tossed it and the plate out the window into the back herb garden. He'd forgotten it was there. With the offensive plate dealt with, the young man rubbed his head and then unbuckled his belt. He dropped it upon the floor, wriggled out of his trousers, then flopped onto the bed which creaked in protest.

Yoder rested his head on his pillow and watched the flickering light dance on the ceiling. He imagined mythical monsters to slay. He dreamed himself a glorious hero with long, golden hair and gleaming plated armor. There was a beautiful, pale-skinned, black-haired girl in virginal white caught in his shield arm. Her body pressed close so he could smell the scent of her long, silky hair. He sighed, adjusted his under-linens, and… well, we'll not go into what he did next.

The night passed. Crickets played their violin legs in the brush. Owls hooted their night song between swooping dives onto unsuspecting critters in the grass. Wolves howled in the forests far, far away, and a man in a very fine short, brim hat of blackened felt tripped on a root. He stumbled, flailing his arms and whacking himself in the knee with the ironwood cane in his left hand. At its top rested a white crystal, cut and fixed with silver brackets in a five-point pattern.

"Ow! Blast you, flora." The man in the felt hat remarked. His expressive face of long, pointed chin and high cheekbones scowled. He turned with a flutter of his woolen, darkened blue long coat tails. "You scuffed my boots!" The man exclaimed, then lifted a gloved hand and raised his index finger to shush the ground.

"Quiet!" he whispered, the same hand brushing off brown road-weary trousers a moment later. "I know I'm a stranger, but it's very rude to trip strangers." He said next, straightening himself up and adjusting both his vest of black and his shirt of white.

"There's a young man in this region with a very serious destiny, an important one, and I intend to find him. No shrubbery roots are going to stop me, thank you very much." The man in the hat explained to the night air, which didn't seem all that concerned about it. This was fine. The fop pressed on with a twirl of his cane, strolling onward toward the sleepy hamlet of Mater's Range once more.

And so, that bright sunny morning began. Yoder Hals rose from his bed and scratched himself forward, then backward. He yawned, trudging to his dresser to pick out yet another blue tunic and dark trousers to wear from the messy clumps within. Soon, his nose was treated to the scent of fresh baking bread and sizzling pork. He wiped the drool from the corner of his mouth. Thumbs pressed to his eyes to clean those little flecks of sleep grit from them. Finally, he pulled each item on to replace those soiled by yesterday. Yesterday's garments were tossed down to the common room floor. As was his tradition, he put on his belt and sat himself down on his creaky bed to pull on his boots.

"Come on down, dear. Breakfast is ready," called his mother. Yoder descended but found himself distracted by a rap-tap tapping upon the front door. He stared at the wooden rectangle, blonde brows furrowing. His sleepy mind could not comprehend who might come to call at such an hour. "Who could that be? Interrupting breakfast." Doreen asked.

Yoder looked at his mother, then the table where his hearty breakfast awaited him. Eggs and sizzled Ham with leftover boiled beans. He licked his lips, looked back at the front door, and decided that the visitor didn't matter. His mother, however, decided the opposite, and the two passed each other by in favor of the other.

"Leave it, mum," Yoder said, rounding the table and sitting down in his spot in front of his plate to take up his knife and fork.

Doreen answered the door, though, ignoring her son. She pulled it wide and brushed a hand through her stringy, unkempt, blonde hair. Her gentle blue eyes fixed on the man in the black felt hat and dark blue long coat. He smiled, full of pearly teeth.

"Hello! Do you have a moment to talk about the savior of all mankind?" The man in the hat said, his sharp, aristocratic features bright and cheery even at this early hour. He swapped his cane from left hand to right hand, holding the left hand out to the woman in the doorway.

"What's this then? Bit early for a Genovan Witness, isn't it?" Doreen replied with veiled disgust showing in a curled sneer. "Serves me right to answer the door at this bloody bell." She snarked at him, dissolving his cheer into surprise and alarm.

"What?" The man in the hat asked, neck craning forward to bring his face closer to slapping range. "No! Goodness, no, ma'am. I'm not a witness. Well, I am but not one of those. I am…" He twirled his crystal-headed cane then put the tip down in front of him. "…The Wizard."

Doreen did not seem impressed, fixing this interruptor with a scathing glare. "Who?

The Wizard cocked an eyebrow then let out a sigh. "The Wizard, ma'am." To which Doreen rolled her blue eyes.

"I heard you the bleedin' first time. You're a Wizard, that's nice. The Wizard of What?" She asked in a huffy tone, hoping this man would get on with it.

"Yes." The Wizard replied, adjusting his coat lapel with the unshaken hand. "I've come for your son, ma'am. A great and powerful destiny awaits him." Doreen stared, her eyes narrowing to squinty slits as she considered this news.

On the one hand, Doreen could slam the door in this upstart's face and be done with it. She could go back to baking and washing her son's clothes, feeding him day in and day out like a good mother should. On the other hand, a small sliver of selfishness jumped at the opportunity. If he went on this great and powerful destiny quest with this foppish prat, then she would be free. She could do whatever she pleased. And oh, the fame of being the mother to a destined youth made her dream of freedom.

Her eyes softened. "Well, why didn't you say so? Come in, come in. Would you like some breakfast, good Sir? I'm so sorry for the rudeness, it's very early and I am knackered." She laughed, stepping aside and gesturing for the strange man in his fine clothes to come in.

"I thank you, ma'am. No doubt your strapping young lad is eager to see the great, wide world, eh? Save humanity, yeah?" The Wizard smiled once more, bowing his head. He swept inside the small house with its thatched roof and looked about at its simplicity. "And what a humble upbringing. Ohhh, yessss. Perfect, exactly as foretold. A modest young life of labor and happiness."

Doreen laughed too, but for different reasons. "I don't know about all that, sir. We just live the life we're given, don't we?" She replied, passing the man by to return to her ovens where the day's baking was getting started. Yoder shoveled eggs and beans into his mouth, ignoring the pointless conversation. The Wizard pulled the felt hat off his head, letting his mop of brown hair free to fall in front of his eyes.

"Too true, ma'am. Too true. And unfortunate, that. Tiny lives or something. I'd wax philosophical, but I'm a bit pressed for time." He looked to the table, expecting a strong young man ready to take up the sword and shield and slay dragons. What he saw was a slovenly, rotund lad with bean juice dripping down his chin. The Wizard frowned, and Yoder frowned right back at him.

"What?" The young man said, mouth full of boiled beans.

"This is…. wait a minute, no. Shut up." The Wizard said, turning away while tucking his hat under his arm. He rummaged through his pockets, producing a scroll that somehow fit in there, and unrolled it. His eyes skimmed the elegant lettering, fixed about the middle, then he rolled it back up. It tucked back away just as improbably. "Well, I suppose…. that's it." Inhaling sharply, the Wizard turned back around to face the boy and his mother with a painted-on smile.

"Fantastic! You, my boy, are chosen by God to quest with me for the betterment of all mankind!" The Wizard announced as best he could muster, arms extending wide for full dramatic scale.

Yoder swallowed his beans, fixed the strange man with a strange look, and replied, "What? You're off your rocker. Who are you supposed to be?"

The Wizard's painted smile cracked. He stared at this unfit and wholly unheroic boy dripping bean juice on his tunic. He tried to keep the corners of his lips up but could feel the muscles trying to pull themselves down.

"Me? I'm The Wizard. Your guide and mentor on this magical crusade."

Yoder screwed his face up in dismay. "The Wizard? The Wizard of What?"

"Yes," he replied to the boy, nodding. "Finish up. Have you got a sword?" The Wizard asked next. Yoder thought for a moment of the blade under his bed and nodded back.

"Yes, upstairs. Why?"

The Wizard smiled. "Excellent, strap it on and meet me outside."

Yoder put his fork down, growing annoyed. "No! And I'm not following some strange man on some mad quest, neither. I'm going to finish my breakfast and go out like I always do, and you can piss off."

The Wizard sighed, all the wind blowing out of his sails. "Boy, the fate of the world lies in your…. capable…. hands. The prophecy was very clear. Your destiny awaits you."

Yoder glanced down at his plate, scratching his cheek with his right hand. He lifted his gaze to the strange man interrupting his breakfast. "Is this really necessary? I mean, I like it here. There's food and my mum," he said, hiding his wringing hands under the table.

The Wizard didn't seem to like that question, shuffling forward to lean down and put his hands and cane on the table. "Are you telling me that you won't go on an epic adventure with me to save the whole of the world because of your mum?" His brown eyes flicked to the aforementioned mother, who looked back from her oven with a frown. "No offense, ma'am. You're lovely, really."

Yoder swallowed a lump in his throat. Fear had always been a constant companion. Now more than ever, he was certain that leaving the safety and security of home was a very bad idea. However, this strange man also presented him with everything he'd ever dreamed about. Adventure, destiny, perhaps even a pale maiden with dark hair or two.

"Well, I mean, no. I… I don't know, it's going to be dangerous, isn't it?" Yoder stammered.

"Oh yes, very. Incredibly dangerous, potentially deadly, and full of the worst wonders you could dream of." The Wizard replied. "It'll be brilliant fun," he added with a smile, pushing back upright off the table.

"I'll be right outside when you're ready." The Wizard said in the ensuing awkward silence. Yoder's unseen hands rubbed over each other like a rat cleaning his claws. He contemplated if the cheese in the trap was worth the risk.

"Sorry," The Wizard offered after turning away to leave but turning back again. "What's your name, lad?" He asked.

Yoder tried not to turn sheet white, smacking his lips as his mouth had gone dry. "Y-Yoder, sir." He mumbled.

The Wizard reared back as if the word were something disgusting. "Yoder? Really? Yoder." He stole a glance at Doreen, who was glaring at him. She reached for her rolling pin. The Wizard chose to backpedal a bit by word and act. "Ohh, lovely name. Majestic, truly. Top-notch. Songs will be sung in drinking halls throughout the realms of…. Yoder." The Wizard coughed, so the name wouldn't make him laugh. He backed up to the door before he made the hastiest of retreats out into the sunny morning air.

Yoder looked at his mother, his mother looked at him, then both eyed the door for a moment when it closed. Destiny had come for Yoder Hals, a boy with little more than fear in his heart. The strange Wizard waited outside and reviewed his scroll. It presented the boy with an opportunity. One that didn't come for anyone, either. Yoder wondered if he could do it, save the world, become the hero he'd always wanted to be, or would he mess up? Get himself killed? Doom the world to darkness.

Doreen put her right hand on her hip, tilted her head, and gave in to the selfishness. "I think you should go. Might as well, right? Big adventure. Savior of humanity. Gets you out of the house, doesn't it?

"MUM!" said Yoder, looking back at his mother with wide, terrified eyes. Doreen shook her head, waving her left hand about like she was swatting a gnat.

"What? It's not every day this sort of thing happens, is it? Daft wizard comes round asking you on a magic quest. Honestly, you're a fool to say No."

Yoder groaned, hanging his head. "Fine. I'll go."

"Let me pack you a lunch then, can't save the world on an empty stomach," his mother replied, turning to the oven with a secret smile on her face.

Chapter Two:
Poppycock's a funny word

The people of Mater's Range went about their daily lives, bustling in the fields or down to the river to wash their linens. The Wizard tucked his cane into his pocket, where it somehow fit. He withdrew the scroll instead. He unrolled it, looking over the elegant ancient text to double check, triple check even, the script.

"Fantastic," he said to himself, rolling the scroll back up and tucking it away once more. An old woman shuffled by pushing a cart of feed and the Wizard bowed to her.

"Madam," he said, to which the old woman made a hissing noise that startled him as she went on her way. "My word! How rude." He commented to himself, but let it go and clasped his hands behind his back to wait.

An hour passed. The Wizard occupied himself by first pacing, then sitting. Finally, he played a game of hopscotch with an imaginary diagram. With one foot up and the other hopping this way and that, The Wizard paused when Yoder opened the door.

The boy stood there, wearing a wool cloak about his shoulders of russet brown and a pack upon his back underneath it. His father's sword was tied to his belt and dangled along his right thigh. The Wizard looked up, met Yoder's surprised expression, and summarily put his foot down.

"You left or right-handed, lad?" he asked, standing up tall and proud like he wasn't hopping about a moment ago.

"Um. Right?" Yoder replied in confusion, fidgeting with his feet as he wondered if he was dressed for an epic quest. He'd always imagined wearing heavy armor, of course. The Wizard chuckled.

"Draw your sword then," he said, leaving Yoder blinking.

"What?"

The Wizard walked toward the corpulent boy. "Draw. Your. Sword." He commanded with a strong tone.

Yoder reached for the grip of the sword with his right hand. He trembled and tried to pull the blade from its wooden scabbard underhanded. The Wizard lifted his left hand and slapped Yoder across his jowled cheek. The sting of the slap made the boy's head jerk, tears beginning to well in his eyes.

"What'd you do that for?!" He cried out.

The Wizard sighed. "If you intend to draw your sword with your right hand and not die before you can get it out, tie it to your left side. Reach across yourself and draw, letting you attack or defend immediately. Go on," he said, stepping back to give the boy room. Yoder sniffled.

"You didn't have to hit me," he muttered, sliding the blade down into the sheath. He untied and affixed it to the left side of his belt at his leg this time. He looked at The Wizard then, reached across himself and grasped the leather grip once more. The blade drew free with a musical scraping sound.

"Wow!" exclaimed Yoder, wide-eyed and amazed as he looked at the shining blade in his hand. The edge was dull, but the metal was beautifully crafted and emblazoned with the etching of a pack of wolves in full gallop down the blade's length. Yoder began to swing the sword about, making childish "shing" noises. The Wizard stepped back even further to avoid getting hit.

"Stop that. Stop it. You're going to stab your eye out," he chided the youth, who frowned and fumbled the tip back into the scabbard then slid it inside.

"Come along, Yoder. We've no time to lose." The Wizard said, rolling his eyes. "Your journey begins today! A grand and magnificent quest to the dark recesses of the Razor's Teeth far, far away. We shall travel to the Trading Post of Galarion's Hollow to provision and then make our way through the Wastes of Kurn. Danger lurks around every rock and tree; the road goes ever onward in our valiant-"

Yoder cut him off, clearing his throat. "Thought you said we've no time to lose…," The boy mentioned, leaving The Wizard glowering at him. "Sorry…," he added, looking down like a whipped pup.

The Wizard harrumphed. He turned on a haughty heel and started marching down the dirt roadway toward the edge of town. Yoder struggled to catch up, panting with only the short sprint that brought him to The Wizard's side.

"Sorry…. huff…. sorry, you said Kurn." Yoder stammered, catching his breath with labored effort. The Wizard smiled, walking at a brisk pace without a care.

"That I did, my boy. For between us and the mountains lie the Wastes, so that is where we shall go."

Yoder swallowed the ever-present lump in his throat. "But that's the land of the Black Vanguard, sir. They'll kill us. I hear they kill you just for the clothes on your back."

The Wizard nodded. "That is true. I mentioned danger, didn't I?" He glanced at the sweating boy beside him, trying to hide his dismay. Yoder groaned; his footsteps became more like the forced march of a child told to go clean his room.

"I don't want to go to Kurn."

"I don't want to take a sniveling child on a magical journey, but the world is doomed if I do not so here I am. Chin up, boy. We all must do things we don't want to do." The Wizard retorted with a sigh, keeping his pace along the dirt road toward the forest between Mater's Range and Galarion's Hollow to the Northeast. Yoder scowled.

"I'm not a sniveling child! I'm a man!" He protested in the most nasal tone possible, like nails on a chalkboard. The Wizard reached into his pocket and withdrew his cane from its mystical depths. He resumed his pace with a step-step-clack rhythm.

Yoder sulked at his side, shuffling his fat feet in those worn boots to keep up with the lanky magician. In time, he got over himself and asked. "How do you do that? Is your pocket magic?"

The Wizard looked at his companion. "Do what?" he asked in reply.

"Put things in there that shouldn't fit?"

The Wizard smiled, nodding. "Ah. Yes. It makes travel quite easy, anything I could ever need right here in my pockets." he added, patting one with his free hand. Yoder smiled, eyes lighting up.

"Could you make my backpack do that?" Dreaming of keeping lots of food, a tent, a bed, even his shiny metal armor when he got it in there.

The Wizard laughed. "I could, yes."

Yoder beamed, eyebrows lifting. "Would you?"

The Wizard smiled, waited a moment for dramatic effect and spoke. "No."

The two now walked in silence. The Wizard step-step-clacked along the path into the forest. Yoder kicked rocks and muttered under his breath about hating wizards and epic quests and leaving his home and his mom. He did so much grumbling that he didn't notice the fields had turned to random rows of trees and the sunshine faded to shade. He groused so hard that he didn't even notice the bend in the path. His head angled down, and his eyes were stuck on his trudging boots instead of the dirt that gave way to grass. So wrapped up in his own misery was he that he walked straight into a tree, the top of his head thunking against the trunk.

"OW!" Yoder cried out, slapping a hand on his bruised noggin which only made the pain worse.

Ten paces to the left, The Wizard stopped. He turned around to find the tubby boy rubbing his crown and looking up at the tree he'd banged into.

"Pay attention!" The Wizard snapped, shaking his head.

Yoder turned his head, looking over at his guide so far away and he turned to waddle towards him. Yoder would've started muttering again, but for a twinkling laughter that rose from the branches above.

"Stupid, fat, human." A gentle voice filled with mirth said, echoing through the foliage.

"I'm not stupid!" Yoder argued in that nasal tone, looking up at the copse of branches above him with a scowl. "I wasn't… paying attention." He explained, which raised more twinkling laughter.

"Stop it! Stop laughing at me!" Yoder bellowed, but the chime-like amusement still lingered around them. The Wizard put his face in his hand, shaking his head as his ward went on a tantrum and he didn't take it out until Yoder let out a strange cry. Half gasp, half gurgle. The Wizard pulled his hand down, raising his cane like a weapon only to find a small creature sitting on the top of Yoder's head.

It was thin and long, colored in shimmering, tiny scales like a rainbow from head to toe. A long tail that ended in a tiny barb whipped about behind it. A lizard-like creature with a lizard-like head and glowing purple eyes. It was no bigger than a house cat.

From its back protruded two billowing wings, like butterflies. They were somewhat transparent and in the same shimmery manner as the scales. The dim light of the forest made each wing take on a cascade of colors. Its rump sat on the very top of Yoder's head, back legs tucked in.

The creature's back curved upward while its front claws balanced on Yoder's hairline. Its long neck was curved upward too, giving the creature a noble Aire. Its tail curled down the back of Yoder's head, so the barb rested on his shoulder near the poor boy's exposed neck. Yoder stood very still, but his face creased in horror and fear with a wide lipped frown. Tears once more started to well in his blue eyes.

The tiny dragon craned its long neck downward, twisting it around so it was looking Yoder in his wide, terrified eyes. "Helloooo. You're funny. Why are your eyes leaking?" It said, a tiny mouth full of sharp, little teeth opening and closing with the words.

Yoder twitched, trembling and going cross-eyed to look at the small face in front of him. He squeaked rather than speak, very much reaching critical fear. The Wizard lowered his cane, moving closer.

"Faerie Dragon. What is your name?" he asked, holding a hand up for The Wizard understood the danger of the little dragon's tail-barb so close to the mewling teen's neck. The lizard-like head drew back from Yoder's face, turning as it lifted its long neck to regard the human with the cane.

"Perrrrrrixstar." The creature purred, tiny scales bristling down its long neck. "I claim this fat human as my slave."

The Wizard's worried expression eased into a smile, but Yoder sputtered spittle from his lips before protesting.

"I'm no one's slave!" He whined, summoning every drop of courage he had to put his foot down. His eyes crossed and swiveled upward toward his brow-line. "Get off my head!"

Both Wizard and dragon laughed, one deeply and the other was like jingling bells. Yoder scowled at The Wizard, who laughed more and beckoned him onward.

"I'm not taking a single step until this thing gets off me!" Yoder called out, holding onto his tiny sliver of courage out of fear of what the little beast might do. Perrixstar padded about in Yoder's hair, shifting its bulk until it could curl up and settle down to rest there.

"Onward, fat slave," the tiny dragon commanded, thwapping the back of Yoder's head with its curled tail. Yoder flinched, growing angrier.

"I mean it! I'm not moving!" He bellowed, but The Wizard had already turned away. He started walking up the road through the forest once more. He did not look back, but twirled his cane between his fingers then resumed his steady step-step-clacking pace.

"You hear me?! Not one step!" Yoder bellowed at The Wizard's back, but the further the man in the short-brimmed hat got; the less sure Yoder became. He swallowed, glancing around him at the dense brush and trees. The faerie dragon on his head curled its neck and rested its head on its own hind leg. Yoder broke, huffing and jogging with great effort to catch up.

He made it to The Wizard's back before his breath gave out and he heaved for air, sweat pouring down his face again. "Do you… huff … have to walk …puff ….so fast?" he complained.

The Wizard chuckled, looking over his shoulder. "Keep up, you can do it. I'd be careful though. Faerie Dragons are gentle creatures but their stinger, that sharp point on the end of the tail, has a potent poison."

Yoder blinked, jowled face aghast. "Seriously??"

The Wizard nodded once. Yoder became very aware of the deadly tail hanging off the back of his skull. He tried very hard to keep his head and neck quite still as he walked behind the Wizard who grinned to himself. All the while, the little dragon slumbered peacefully.

The two traveled through the forest on the road as the sun crested the sky. The Wizard ignored Yoder's complaints until noontime, and he finally relented to the thirtieth request to stop and rest.

"Yes, yes. Alright," he said, stepping off the road to climb a large stone and sit down upon it. Yoder tried to climb up as well, keeping his head very still so as not to disturb the sleeping dragon still curled up on it. His foot slipped, sliding off the side. He caught himself before falling forward and waking the dangerous beast. Upon his second attempt, he crested the stone and sat down beside The Wizard.

"Whew. How much farther is it to Galarion's Hollow?" the boy asked, unstrapping his pack and pulling it around to sit in his lap.

"Half a day." The Wizard replied, resting his cane beside him then taking his hat off his head to fan himself with it. "IF we don't stop every bell's toll to rest and snack."

Yoder frowned at the side-glance The Wizard gave him. "I'm hungry!" He complained, opening his pack to pull out a large sandwich wrapped in cloth. He unwrapped it on the pack. His mouth watered before he even saw the two thick slices of freshly baked bread, generous pieces of ham and cut cheese with lettuce and tomato providing a rich splash of color.

It was even cut by his mother before she wrapped it, sliced into two isosceles triangles. Yoder smiled, reminded of his mother back home. It became bittersweet, thinking that he was half a day away from everything that was comfortable and safe. That this was the last of his mother's homemade sandwiches he would eat for a long, long time.

The Wizard watched the boy, sympathizing. He lifted a hand, reached over and snatched one of the sandwich triangles off the cloth. Yoder's head swung about, looking from lone sandwich triangle to Wizard and back and forth again.

"Wh-Hey! That's…" But before he could finish the sentence, The Wizard took a hefty bite off the point and began to chew. Yoder scowled.

"Sure, great. Enjoy," he said bitterly. The Wizard replied with a squirrel cheeked smile, toasting the boy with the rest of the sandwich. He chewed crisp vegetables, sweet and salty ham and soft bread. Yoder sighed, picked up his remaining half and opened his mouth wide to take a bite only for the barbed tail of Perrixstar to flick down into his visual range. He stopped, going still.

Perrixstar yawned, lifting its long neck while the stinger tip dangled in front of Yoder's eyes. It stood up, back arching high in a stretch that fanned its great wings out wide before they folded back down along its back once more. "Ohhhhh! Is it lunchtime? Feed me, fat slave," the creature purred, swinging its stinger back and forth in lazy threat. Yoder gulped, shifting a trembling hand off the sandwich.

"B-but it's my l-last half…," he said, sad and frightened. Perrixstar's long, reptilian tongue flicked out of its mouth and licked at its maw-rim.

"Now" It threatened in a firm but musical tone. "Give me sweet meat."

The Wizard swallowed his mouthful, chuckling. He watched the mythic beast and boy interact while Yoder picked out a piece of ham from his sandwich and held it up over his head. The boy's fingers trembled, making the ham wiggle.

The dragon lifted its head up toward the thick piece of ham held up. Its neck undulated from its torso all the way up to its tiny head. It opened its mouth wide to fire out a small gout of flame that singed the meat. Its head snapped forward lightning-quick like a snake, catching the burned meat as Yoder cried out. He let go, pulling his hand down to his mouth. His finger and thumb were both singed black, stinging like when one touches a hot pan without gloves.

"Owwwww!" Yoder moaned, sticking both fingers in his mouth to suck on them. Perrixstar retracted his neck and curled back up on Yoder's head to eat with snapping teeth and strong swallowing. Yoder pulled his fingers from his mouth with a wet pop.

"That's it! I'm done being your slave!" He announced angrily, shaking his hand about to try and stop the burning ache in the two tips. "Get off my head!"

"No." Perrixstar replied after a bite of ham made it all the way down its throat. It retracted the barbed tail, curling its tail around itself as it ate. The Wizard laughed between his own bites, chewing and shaking his head. Yoder was displeased.

He'd not even gotten to eat his own sandwich yet, half of it stolen. His fingertips were scorched by an annoying pest that wouldn't leave him be. He grumbled, finally taking a bite of what was left of his mother's homemade sandwich. The sweet meat and juicy vegetables burst in his mouth, tempered by the delicious, dry bread.

His eyes closed. He forgot about his aching fingers as he was taken back to lazy days sitting at his table at home, having lunch without a care in the world. Not even the threat of Faerie Dragon sting could dull the comfort of his mom's fresh lunch. His reverie was broken by the sound of horses whinnying and galloping. A cart creaked as four riders rode by them up the road from the same direction they'd come. Yoder opened his eyes to watch them escort the covered cart by. Each one was travel-worn, their armor and hooded cloaks dusty and dirty.

Some wore swords, others carried bows. The driver of the cart had a large two-handed axe beside him. His hood rode high to hide his face and he had his cloak wrapped firmly around him save for his arms guiding the reins. They flicked now and then, spurring the horses onward. On the other side of the axe was a young girl, no older than Yoder. Fair of skin and thin, she wore a brown tunic and green cloak with the hood down. Her hair sun-kissed brown and fluttering in the wind of hasty travel. She looked content.

"Who are they?" Yoder asked, watching the pretty girl as best he could as she and her companions sped by. The Wizard shrugged.

"Adventurers, most likely. Plenty of those about, heavily armed and too violent to be helpful. They're as bad as beasts, really. Get a group of them together and they will murder every living thing in a dungeon or cavern purely for what they can scavenge off of them. It's an odd economic system, we have. I tried to tell the council that setting up a meritocratic financial stratagem based on killing was a bad idea. Poppycock, Reisland said." The Wizard grunted, popping the last piece of sandwich into his mouth to chew. Yoder laughed childishly and The Wizard frowned at him.

"What?"

"Poppycock's a funny word," Yoder explained, almost giggling immaturely.

The Wizard rolled his brown eyes. "Oh, shut up." He swatted the boy with his felt hat but found himself chuckling anyways as one tended to do when someone else laughed at something stupidly.

Chapter Three:
Don't Tell Me What to Do

Many hours of walking and complaining later, The Wizard, Yoder, and Yoder's new master stepped clear of the forest to look upon Galarion's Hollow. Yoder could scarcely believe his eyes, wide with awe at the large settlement nestled in a cleft valley. Yoder was surprised when The Wizard pointed it out and all he saw were small buildings like huts with pointed metal spires protruding from the roof.

As they drew closer in the dying light of the day, he realized that the entire town, almost a city, was settled in a valley and the small huts were actually the tiptops of tall, towering buildings made of stone and wood far, far below. So far below that Yoder grew dizzy peering over the edge of the valley and so decided not to do that anymore.

The Wizard called to him, beckoning with a wave for the youth to follow as he walked along the trail at the edge of the rocks to where a ladder guarded by two strong and vicious looking men awaited. The ladder led down to a platform and that platform held both a lift made with pulleys and rope as well as a rope bridge from one side of the valley wall to the other where a similar platform waited over there. Yoder eyed the two guards suspiciously as they approached, watching the men banter back and forth only to fall silent and stare at the travelers wickedly.

"Oi! Stand to!" One called out, holding up his left hand while his right reached for the dagger at his belt.

The Wizard raised his cane and shook it like he was waving. "Here be weary travelers, come to drown their sorrows," he said lyrically, lowering the cane and standing still. Yoder stepped up behind him, Faerie Dragon still curled up but quite alert on top of his head. The speaking guard nodded once.

"Then be ye welcome ta Galarion's Hollow," he replied gruffly, motioning now with his halting hand for them to pass. The Wizard did so, cheerily strolling between the two with Yoder close on his coattails like a child hiding in his mother's skirt. The guards eyed Yoder's head or rather the beast upon it, then looked at each other to confirm they both had actually seen it but neither felt inclined to say anything.

The Wizard chose the lift, stepping into the huge platform's fenced circumference then he turned and leaned against the rail to wait for Yoder. The boy seemed once more suspicious of this device like everything else, stepping carefully onto it and immediately grasping the fence as soon as it shook slightly. The Wizard chuckled, waving his cane at the pulley rope while Yoder inspected the many slats of wood that made up the floor. One could easily fit a cart and horses on this thing, but he reasoned that would be silly. The weight alone would bring the lift crashing down, he assumed. Carts were very heavy, as were horses.

Suddenly, the platform began to shake and descend. Yoder yelped and clung harder to the wooden beams that made up the circling fence. He felt dizzy again, closing his eyes but The Wizard cleared his throat and spoke. "Look, boy. Look." When Yoder opened his eyes and truly looked around, he was amazed by all that Galarion's Hollow was.

Small rope bridges crisscrossed from building to building, some with laundry hanging off them and others with decorations. Lighted lanterns, flags, kites, and more than one pair of laced boots dangled off the hand-ropes. People milled to and fro along them as though the height and risk of falling weren't even a thought. But the most spectacular part of the hidden village was the buildings themselves. Tall and sturdily built, Yoder looked over the structures with huge doors instead of windows that let people in and out as much as they cooled the rooms within.

Down, down, the platform descended, carrying the three visitors all the way to the bottom where the streets of Galarion's Hollow were packed full of small shops peddling anything and everything. "This used to be a smuggler's den many, many full cycles passed, operated by the notorious thief Galarion Nightrunner. His guild, the Nightrunners still keep the peace and enforce the laws of the Hollow to this day. The leader of the Nightrunners acts as both Guild Boss and de facto Mayor."

Yoder barely heard him, so enamored with the busy, alien place that he stopped thinking about descending and only realized they were settled on the bottom when The Wizard pushed off the rail and walked out down the ramp. "Come along, come along." He bid the boy who followed quickly to keep up. The smell of cooking meat caught his nose, and his mouth began to water, so too did the Faerie Dragon's above him. Perrixstar's head flicked this way and that, scenting the food and looking about the strange, human gathering place.

The main thoroughfare was a buzzing hive of activity, people coming and going up and down the dirt road. Some with horses or pack-beasts, some driving carts which people parted around only to close back in behind them like a river's stream around a stone. Peddlers and vendors bellowed about their wares, offering fresh meats both cooked and raw, rare curios, weapons, armor, pottery, and jewelry. Yoder nudged The Wizard as they walked down the street.

"Is this where we buy me my suit of armor?" he asked with bright, hopeful blue eyes. The Wizard didn't seem to appreciate being jostled, scowling at the touch before he shook his head.

"Who said we were buying you armor?" he asked with a raised brow. Yoder's hope died, his shoulders sagging.

"But I'm the hero, right? A hero needs armor to protect himself while he slays dragons and saves the world!"

Perrixstar whapped the back of Yoder's head, hissing down at him. Yoder flinched, raising his hands to instinctively reach for the spot he was thumped on but changed his mind and lowered them again. "Sorry. I'm just saying, I don't want to die." The Wizard laughed.

"That's true, if you die then the prophecy goes unfulfilled. I suppose we should gird you then."

Yoder's face lit up. "Ohhh, thank God," he laughed nervously, looking away for a moment to listen and locate one of the armor peddlers. "I think I heard an armorer nearby…" He said, looking back to find The Wizard gone. Yoder blinked, turning this way and that way and all around himself which made the dragon on his head chirp in amusement at the game.

"Wheee! Again!" It cheered while Yoder began to sweat, breathing faster and faster.

"Where…Sir?! W-Wizard!? Oh God." His heart began to pound in his chest, terror gripping him as the hustle and bustle stopped being wondrous and became a frightening clamor.

So loud, so chaotic. People pushed past him, jostling him about like a leaf in the wind. "Wheeee!" cheered the little dragon, swaying its long neck back and forth so its head wobbled to and fro happily. "I need…. I need…." Yoder stammered to himself, looking about with wild eyes until he saw a sign. "Fletch and Flicker's Tavern!" He'd heard stories, even stepped into the tavern back home once though he didn't stay long out of fear one of the men who spent their time there would chastise him. Yoder pushed through the crowd and then the door, stumbling a step inside the drinking hall.

Fletch and Flicker's was a huge common area of wooden floors and stone walls that made up the base of one of the towering structures, where the many seats and tables were filled with people drinking, carousing, playing games of chance, and dining on cooked meats and fresh breads as well as nuts and fruits. Yoder looked around, catching his breath with a hand on his heart. A pretty maid in a long, burgundy dress and apron gracefully floated by him, an empty tankard dangling from one finger of her hand.

"You okay, sweetling?" she asked loudly but kindly. "You look like you might die of fright." Yoder stared at her with wide eyes, having interacted with women very little other than his mother.

"Uhh...y-yes. H-Hi," he mumbled.

The barmaid smiled softly. "Come on in, honey. You got coin?" she asked, glancing at the packed bar and then around the expansive hall until she found a bench unoccupied off in the corner.

"Uhh. Yes. Some." Yoder said.

The maid smiled more. "Follow me then, I'll get you a drink and a nice bowl of soup to warm your belly." The maternal nature soothed Yoder, who followed the woman over to the corner bench where he sat down. The maid motioned with the tankard toward the little dragon on his head. "Does that need to eat too?" She asked. Perrixstar wiggled its neck excitedly.

"Yes. Feed me, human female slave." It replied eagerly.

Yoder sighed. "Don't mind it, it thinks all humans are its slaves. A piece of meat for it too." The maid laughed softly, nodding and dancing away to put in the order.

Yoder waited, sitting on the bench in the corner and looked around the tavern's common area. His blue eyes moved from face to grizzled face until he noticed the pretty girl from the caravan early that day. She was laughing with a group of large men, presumably the ones she had ridden with before. He watched her toast with a mug of ale bigger than her head then tipped it back and began to gulp down the contents along with the others. It amazed him, how someone so small and dainty-looking could drink with such large and aggressive men.

The Barmaid returned with a small serving dish bearing two pieces of roasted beef on top and a bowl of hot, steaming, chicken soup. Yoder took the bowl eagerly, his stomach already growling with hunger, but he looked up at the woman with the small dish of meat curiously as she hovered. She was holding a piece of beef between two of her slender fingers and sort of waving it in Perrixstar's general direction as if she were afraid but unwilling to not do her job to its fullest either.

Yoder smiled. "Just…. put the dish on my head. You really don't want to be anywhere near the meat when its hungry." The maid looked surprised, gingerly sliding the small dish onto Yoder's skull. Perrixstar's tail swung around and encircled it to hold it still.

"Thank you, human slave," It purred graciously…. for a faerie dragon anyways.

"That'll be half a silver, sweetheart," The barmaid asked, holding her hand out. Yoder put the bowl of soup aside, untethered his pack from his back while Perrixstar incinerated the meat on the dish which caused the maid to twitch, startled. In truth, the small gout of flame got practically everyone's attention, but Yoder didn't even notice while he intently rummaged within the backpack till, he found his coin purse. He opened it, withdrew seven copper coins and cupped them in his fist. He looked up, holding the money out to the woman.

"Here you go, thank you. There's a little more for being so kind. It's been a weird day. Is something burning?" Yoder asked, for an acrid scent had caught his nose. The barmaid giggled, taking the coins and pointing to the dragon or rather the singed hairs around the dish the dragon clutched on Yoder's head that he couldn't see.

"What?" Yoder frowned, but then a look of horror took over his face. "Oh god, did it do the fire thing again?" He looked upward at his brows. "Oi! Stop doing the fire thing on my head!" He whined at the dragon, who ignored him in favor of eating dinner. The maid giggled again, tossing her curly hair over her shoulder.

"If you need anything else, give us a wave." She said, turning away to continue serving the floor. Yoder sighed, picking up his bowl of soup to busy himself with some food in peace. He supported the bowl in one hand carefully, the other hand taking up the large spoon to shovel savory broth, soft, cut vegetables and shreds of chicken in herbs into his mouth. His eyes closed, relishing the taste for a moment while chewing and swallowing.

Yoder opened his eyes after the moment passed only to find the Wizard sitting beside him like he'd been there the whole time. It had only been mere seconds, but somehow the Wizard was relaxed and seated at his side with one leg crossed over the other and his arms crossed upon his knee. He even had an ornate, swoop-curved wooden pipe in his hand that wisped a rich, almost sweet smoke from its bowl. Yoder nearly dropped his soup bowl, but thankfully only spilled some broth before recovering. He squeaked, cleared his throat and then chastised the older man.

"Where've you been? I was worried sick!"

The Wizard smiled. "You asked me for armor, young hero." He replied, leaving Yoder trembling in excitement.

"Where is it?" The boy asked.

The Wizard raised his pipe and puffed on it a few times. "Mm, I suspect in the shop we'll purchase it from. You sound like your mother, you know."

The boy frowned. "I do not." He would've argued further but for the sudden presence of the pretty young woman with the adventuring group's approach. She strode up to the two, put her hands confidently on her slender hips in black trousers despite the simple, basic longsword in its leather sheath at her right hip which Yoder surmised meant she was left-handed and upnod the young man who wished he could eat his soup in peace.

"What's that on your head?" She asked in a voice that was too girlish to be threatening but gruffly tried anyways.

Yoder sighed. "It's a Faerie Dragon and its name is Perrixstar," he explained, so hungry that he wasn't even concerned about the girl's presence.

"Can I pet it?" she asked, holding her chin up proudly as she looked at the fat kid with the bowl of soup. The Wizard beside Yoder chuckled. Yoder shook his head.

"I wouldn't, it's not very nice and its stinger is extremely poisonous," he warned, but the girl seemed unphased. Her booted feet, one of which held a small dagger tucked into the side, stanced wide and squared.

"It's your pet, haven't you trained it? That's stupid."

Yoder scowled. "Great, another one."

Perrixstar lifted its serpentine neck and scaley head to peer at the small female. "I just claimed him." The creature purred. "I am training my fat slave, but he is stupid and slow to learn." Yoder groaned, the girl and The Wizard both laughed then she tilted her head and lifted her left hand to thrust forward.

"Leeni Vex."

Yoder was surprised to find the offered hand aimed at him and not The Wizard. He started to offer her his bowl of soup, but then realized what he was doing and reached out with his free right hand to shake hers.

Now keenly aware that he was talking to a girl, a pretty girl at that, his hand was sweaty and shaky. "Y-oder Hals." He tried to shake firmly, but just ended up awkwardly wiggling her hand in his.

Leeni looked openly disgusted, pulling her hand back and wiping it on her trouser leg. "And you are?" she asked, looking at the refined gentleman with the pipe sitting next to Yoder.

"The Wizard. Charmed." He replied, inclining his head graciously to the girl who frowned.

"The Wizard of What?" Leeni wondered out loud.

"Yes." was The Wizard's reply which only further confused the girl.

Even Yoder looked at his companion funny, opening his mouth to ask why he kept saying that, but the girl interjected. "Why are you two here?"

Yoder saw his chance to impress her and puffed out his chest proudly. "I'm a hero. We're provisioning before we make our way through Kurn to the Razor Teeth mountains." The Wizard smiled, but Leeni seemed unimpressed.

"You?! Pfft. How are you a hero?"

Yoder opened his mouth, about to angrily explain but his bravado faltered as he thought on his retort. "Because! Uh. He said so." Dropping the onus on The Wizard who rolled his eyes and explained.

"Yoder here is destined to save the world from great danger."

Leeni laughed mockingly. "Him?" She looked down at Yoder, who was trying to spoon some soup into his mouth and accidentally dropped the spoon when he looked up.

"What? It's destiny. I'm going to be a legend and you're just some girl in a tavern."

Leeni scowled at him, her lips and eyes tense. "Listen, fat boy. I'm an adventurer and a great one. Me and my men over there..." She turned slightly and pointed at the gruff company she kept, drinking and laughing around their table. "...raided the ruins of Kawanor. Big payday. All you have is a weird wizard and that thing." The Wizard looked up.

"Hey!" Perrixstar hissed at her. "Meatless human slave, I am not a thing."

Yoder even grew angry. It was one thing to make fun of him, but another to make fun of his friends. "Shut up!" He threw down his bowl of soup and rose quickly before the girl. Once he was standing, he realized just how small she was. Barely five feet and thin as a rail, the girl was overshadowed by his great bulk but stood her ground defiantly.

Her eyes narrowed and she hissed through her teeth. "Don't tell me what to do."

"You-You're just a mean, little girl," Yoder said rudely, staring down at her with as much confidence born of anger as he could muster but no real will to back it up.

Leeni tensed, her body going rigid, and she reached for her sword. "Like you're anything but a tubby jerk," she snapped, starting to draw the blade.

The confrontation was drawing attention, eyes began to turn toward the two, but The Wizard sat contentedly on the bench to watch. Yoder and Leeni exchanged insults, some quite barbed and some childish until Leeni had enough and yanked her sword from her scabbard. Yoder stepped back with a yelp and reached for his own blade but as he was drawing the wolf-engraved sword from its wooden sheathe, Leeni's sword tip clanked on the floor in between them.

Yoder looked down at the simple blade, then up at the girl and he noticed her arms were shaking. Leeni clenched her teeth and pulled the sword back up to point it at him, but her arms trembled so hard that she had to let it drop again. The tavern erupted into laughter, especially the table full of Leeni's own "men". Her cheeks flushed red in humiliation and anger. Yoder's expression turned to delight as he pushed his sword back down into its scabbard.

"Ohh, big adventurer you are."

The girl glared at him, her eyes going wet and glistening in the candlelight. She dropped the sword with a thud, stomped her foot and then ran clear out of the tavern before Yoder could even react.

Chapter Four:
I'm the pretty one!

As Leeni escaped the humiliation, Yoder watched, dumbfounded then turned around to look at The Wizard who was puffing at his pipe still. "Can you believe that girl?" he asked, motioning with his hands from the doorway she had fled from to the bowl of soup he'd thrown on the floor.

The Wizard inhaled deeply on his pipe, lowered it to his lap and tilted his head to the left slightly. "Can you?"

Yoder frowned at him, lowering his hands. "I mean, she was so rude!" He'd reply, but his expression softened the more he thought on the exchange. Soon, he began to feel bad for making her cry like that in front of everyone. He'd cried in front of the menfolk of his village once, it was the worst feeling he had ever felt and colored the whole of his life forevermore.

The Wizard watched his young ward's eyes, his thoughtful expression becoming a gentle smile. "There it is," he said to himself as Yoder adjusted his sword belt under his gut.

"I'm going to go talk to her…," he announced.

The Wizard rose up to a stand then situated his pipe to his lips again. "Good lad," he affirmed, following Yoder on his way through the crowd to the exit.

Perrixstar curled back up on Yoder's head, casually flicking its barbed tail once. "Humans." It purred in a most derogatory fashion.

Out in the street, Yoder paused to look around at the busy commotion he'd fearfully fled from. The Wizard was with him this time though and for the time being, he was safe enough. However, there was no sign of the crying girl anywhere. Both Yoder and The Wizard looked from face to face as fast as they could while the processions milled back and forth but none of them were the girl. Yoder sighed, shoulders sagging. "Damn." He said to himself. He closed his blue eyes and thought back to that horrible day in his youth.

He had come to join the men and boys in some rough housing, a playtime he and his father used to engage in before his father passed. As the boys rallied together to face the giants that were their fathers, brothers, and friends, Yoder had come huffing and puffing down from his mother's home to join in the rebellion. All the lads cheered, rushing the men in the center of town and Yoder put his great size to use as boys crashed into men's legs and waists. He'd wrapped his big arms around Uller the Tillman's right leg and heaved so hard that the back of his trousers ripped wide open. Uller, unbeknownst to Yoder, had nearly been toppled by the grab. The boy, while large and flabby, was much stronger than his thinner compatriots at the time.

But the moment his pants split, Yoder yelped and scrambled away to cover his rump with his hands. The play-battle ended in raucous laughter, full of pointing fingers and guffaws that brought the thick, little boy to tears instantly. He felt mocked for wanting to be part of something wonderful, something he had loved since his first moments in this world and so, he cried, and he fled. Not home, he couldn't face his mother. No, he ran around the back of the house and curled himself up under the garden table. There, Yoder the child had sat all day and cried. When the sun set, he slipped inside and lied to his mother about ruining his trousers while he changed.

"I think I know where she is," he said over his shoulder, eyes opening. Yoder began to push through the crowd, turning right and moving near the booths quickly to look for the back of the tavern hall. The Wizard followed, only distracted once or twice along the route by a vendor and a particularly pretty moonbird in a cage. The two slipped between two booths and soon stepped into a darkened accessway between the tavern hall's back wall and the rocky face of the crevasse' border. Yoder slowed, motioning to The Wizard to hang back.

Up ahead, Leeni sat on a crate with her knees drawn up and her arms wrapped tightly around them. Even in the dark, he could see her shoulders shaking. Yoder approached, clearing his throat. "Hey…," he said nervously as Leeni snapped her head up in alarm then glowered at the young man walking toward her.

"Go away, jerk," she said, sniffing both indignantly and sorrowfully.

Yoder shook his head. "No. Look. I'm sorry. Are you okay?" he asked gently, tipping his head to the right. Leeni's glower intensified.

"No, stupid. I'm not okay. I'm crying!" she snapped at him, putting Yoder on the back foot as that word was bandied about again.

"I'm not stupid! Stop saying that!"

Perrixstar shifted on his head, lifting its little head up then shoved the plate off. "Fat Slave doesn't like being called stupid even when he's being stupid," it said.

Yoder was flummoxed, sputtering his lips nonsensically until he finally found words. "Shut up, you!" was the best he could come up with.

Leeni smirked at the exchange, then a small giggle escaped her. She craned her neck curiously, extending one long leg off the crate toward the ground. "Fat Slave is stupid," she said to the dragon on the large youth's head.

Perrixstar unfurled its wings and stretched them high, even in the dark; they shimmered. "No, Fat Slave is only stupid when he's being stupid. Female Slave is too. She lost her sword."

Leeni had reached the ground when the dragon's words stung her, causing her back to stiffen. "Oh DAMMIT!" She cried out, her arms flopping upwards only to crash back down against her hips. They planted there and she adopted that cocky stance of hers again as she eyed Yoder. "This is all your fault."

Yoder groaned. "How is it my fault? You can't even hold it upright. Besides, it's just a sword." He finished with disdain in his tone. Leeni rushed forward with a hand raised to smack him, but skid to a stop when the dragon's tail-barb whipped around the back of Yoder's head in her way. Perrixstar hissed a warning.

"Mine. Get your own fat slave."

The girl pulled her hand back, closed it into a fist then extended her index finger to wave threateningly in Yoder's face which Perrixstar seemed to be fine with. Its tail retracted back behind Yoder's head again. "An adventurer needs a weapon, stupid. I can't make money if I don't have a weapon!"

Yoder shrugged. "So, buy a new one or go find it in the tavern? Maybe it's still there?"

The Wizard called out. "Forgive him, he's a tad sheltered." Which garnered a scathing look from Yoder before he focused on Leeni again. She wagged her finger even harder.

"Stupid! This is the Hollow, it's a free for all around here. I can't believe I let you do this to me, you're such a jerk!"

Yoder had enough, swatting her finger with his meaty hand. "Stop it. It's not my fault! I'm so sick of everyone calling me stupid. I'm not stupid!" He growled, turned away and marched firmly toward The Wizard waiting for him at the end of the crude alley.

Leeni watched him storm away, lowering her hand and pointy finger. "Okay! Okay!" She said in defeat, bouncing boot falls carrying her quickly to catch up to him. "Look, Hero. I'll make a deal with you. You get me a weapon and I'll help you complete your quest or whatever."

Yoder scoffed, feeling empowered for the first time in his life. "You can't even swing a sword, how are you going to help?"

Leeni thought about punching him, but the dragon's threat stayed in her mind, and she grit her teeth instead. "I'm an adventurer…," she reminded him with an angry hiss. "Maybe the sword isn't for me. Fine! How about you help me find one that is, and I'll protect you. I know the roads, the dangers, how to make money AND how to not get fleeced by these greedy merchants around here."

The Wizard chimed in as the two reached him. "That won't be a problem, we'll be shopping the Midnight Bazaar."

Leeni's eyes turned wide as saucers. "Really? That's…. wait, you're the real deal then…," she remarked.

The Wizard smiled and gave an affirming nod. "I'm afraid so."

Leeni brushed her fingers through her wild hair in an effort to tame it or make herself more presentable. "Then you've got to let me come with you. I'll help, I swear."

Yoder scowled. "You just want to get famous and make us buy stuff. I don't care how pretty you are; we don't need you."

Leeni raised a brow, taking hold of the tip of a lock of her hair. She tugged on it gently, twisting it back and forth between her fingers while giving Yoder a coy smile. "You think I'm pretty, hmm?"

Yoder turned ghost white, flapping his lips before he looked away. "N-No! I... uh...was just saying. It's...um…" He glanced at his companion, who tapped out his pipe on the ground and pretended not to notice the silent request for backup. Yoder sighed, growing uncomfortable when Leeni drew closer to him.

"It's okay," she said, saccharine sweet. "I don't mind…," she added, reaching out to touch his shoulder with walking fingertips. "I'll do a-EEK!" Leeni jumped back as Perrixstar's tail-barb whipped at her fingers then spiraled up above its body.

Yoder laughed until the flat of the tail thwapped him in the back of the head. "OW!" He groaned.

Perrixstar hissed, its little lizard head swinging tensely back and forth. "I'm the pretty one. You, don't touch my Fat Slave ever." Its tongue flicked out at Leeni.

"Why'd you hit me then!? I didn't do anything!" Yoder complained.

Perrixstar's neck arched, and its little head floated down into Yoder's view again. "I'M THE PRETTY ONE." it demanded, snapping its tiny maw of sharp teeth at his nose.

Yoder yelped. "Okay! You're pretty!" The dragon pulled its head back up and sat in that reared, regal position on Yoder's head proudly. T

The Wizard laughed, shaking his head. "Are we taking this one with us then?" he asked, nodding to Leeni. Yoder was beside himself with confusion at all that just happened. The first time a girl had been flirty with him -ever- and the dragon on his head demanding that it was more important. His brain felt like it would collapse in on itself, giving him a headache.

"Fine. Whatever. She can come." Yoder finally gave in, tired of arguing and being confused. Leeni grinned, nodding firmly to The Wizard who beckoned them onward back out into the street.

"Follow me, the bazaar should be starting shortly." He said, weaving back into the flow of foot traffic with Yoder, his draconic master, and Leeni in tow. The three walked through Galarion's Hollow all the way down to the Nightrunner's Den, a large gateway entrance into a series of caverns the Nightrunners turned into their base after using it for years as a storehouse.

The Gate was huge and flanked by crude parapets where men in black cloaks stood guard above with crossbows or full bows at the ready. Two guards stood on either side of the heavy wooden gateway's opening.

The Wizard approached the guardsmen, each wearing the black cowl of the Nightrunners with a moon and dagger insignia emblazoned on the top of the hood. He produced a missive from one of his vest pockets instead of his coat, holding it out. One guard checked it then motioned them inside without a word.

Passing through the massive, open gates, Yoder wondered just how long it had taken to construct such a tremendous door. Leeni strode behind Yoder, chest puffed out and arms flexed as firmly as her lithe limbs could get in order to try to look larger and more imposing than her barely five feet and slight build truly was.

The Wizard step-step-clacked onward as the cavernous tunnel opened up even wider to a rounded underground expanse. Shop-stalls were set up in a swirling pattern, starting on Yoder's left and spiraling inward to the center of the cave.

"Wow…" Yoder exclaimed as Leeni stepped up beside him.

"I know, right?" she said. "I've always wanted to come in here, but it's invitation only. They say that only the finest of the finest are sold at the Midnight Bazaar."

The Wizard looked back, smiling. "Tis true. Galarion Nightrunner's greatest achievement, a market of the best of the best where pricing is enforced by the guild. No haggling, but a guaranteed fair value at every stall agreed upon by the merchants who sell here. There are two in particular for both of you to peruse. Dorgrin's Forge and Maltheus' Fittings. We'll visit Dorgrin's first together and find a suitable arm for Miss Leeni, but I'll be leaving you two at the Fittings to conduct some business of my own. Come along."

Yoder and Leeni followed the Wizard, while Perrixstar curled back up on Yoder's head but warily watched everything with its glowing purple gaze. The stall marked Dorgrin's Forge was a large tent filled with racks of weaponry and manned by a thick, brawny, bearded man pockmarked by soot and oils.

The Wizard walked within the racks, calling out. "You call these weapons?! Toothpicks is what they are!"

Dorgrin snapped an angry glare at the foppish man, hiking up his toolbelt around his waist. "Ya call yerself a mage? Trickster's wot you are!" He bellowed, devolving into boisterous laughter as he stomped from behind his sales table and approached The Wizard with arms wide.

"Where the hell've you been?!" The big man asked, giving The Wizard a firm hug that made the smaller man squirm but pat him on his wide back.

"Oh, here and there as usual." The Wizard replied, brushing soot off his finery when the smith stepped back. "I need a weapon for the young lady here, if you please and there's only one man I know who can arm her appropriately. Swords did not work out for her…" Leeni huffed, crossing her arms over her chest.

Dorgrin looked upon the slender girl, stroking his russet beard which his fingers left streaked in black. "Can see why, put some meat on them bird bones, girl. Swords, axes, even most lances're gonna be rough fer ya without some muscle."

Leeni grunted. "I know that!" She snipped, looking away from the critique. Dorgrin smirked.

"Spitfire, this one. Ever considered usin' your size as your advantage? Thinkin' short swords or short blade n' dirk if yer hell bent on melee."

Yoder listened and watched, looking between Dorgrin and Leeni curiously. Leeni seemed to be coming around. A short sword is still a sword and maybe it'd help her get strong enough to wield a full sword one day.

She finally looked at the smith. "Well…let's see what you've got, Hairy." She said with false bravado, which Dorgrin only laughed at. "C'mon, girly. Lemme show ya!" Leeni unfolded her arms and followed the big man, which left Yoder and The Wizard to wait.

Yoder moved to stand by The Wizard, speaking in a low tone to him. "Should I ask him to sharpen my father's sword?"

The Wizard raised a brow, looking at his ward with a mysterious expression on his face. "I think that's a fantastic idea."

Yoder frowned at him, not understanding the look. "What? What'd I do now?" he asked dejectedly, which made The Wizard laugh lightly.

"No, no. I mean it. I was just surprised that you'd thought of it."

Yoder blinked, brightening. "Oh. Yeah?" The Wizard nodded.

Perrixstar purred overhead. "Wizard Slave thinks you're not so stupid now…"

Yoder sighed, but he couldn't help feeling proud for a little while. Perhaps he was learning. The Wizard eyed the dragon on Yoder's head, muttering. "Call me slave again and I'll roast you on a spit."

Perrixstar flicked its tongue at the foppish man. "Fire is friend, Wizard Slave can't roast." The Wizard balked at that, scrunching his face up at the impertinent dragon.

Leeni and Dorgrin returned, Leeni now sporting a wide, tan leather belt on her small hips that sat angled low on the side where her short sword in its sheath rested. A curved dirk was nestled in thong cradle that protected her from the blade's edge on the opposite side, but it was positioned to the front rather than side. She beamed a brilliant, happy smile that Yoder found quite pleasing; his eyebrows lifting in awe.

Dorgrin cast The Wizard an upnod. "Mythric steel short blade n' dirk, lighter weight but sharp enough to kill. Twenty total. On the council's tab then?" He asked, which The Wizard cryptically nodded to but didn't explain even after Leeni and Yoder questioned him with looks.

"Thank you, my friend. As ever."

Dorgrin chuckled, bowing his head. "Glad to, be safe out there!"

But Yoder stepped forward boldly then shrank some as he realized just how large and strong this blacksmith was in comparison to him.

"Uh. I was wondering…. if you might…. uh…. sharpen my sword for me?" He stammered.

Dorgrin smiled. "Aye, lad. I can do that." Yoder exhaled in relief, unbuckling the sheath from his belt to hold out. Dorgrin took it, drew the blade free save for the tip that rested on the mouth of the wooden scabbard. He checked the blade, noted the emblazoned wolves with raised bushy brows. "Wolf's run? Yer Joren's boy?"

Yoder blinked in surprise. "You knew my dad?"

Dorgrin slid the blade back into its sheath. "Aye, made this sword for him. I'll take good care of her. Come round on your way out, she'll be ready."

Yoder wanted to ask a million questions, but The Wizard cleared his throat to interrupt. "We need to keep moving."

The Wizard smiled while Yoder frowned but fell silent, bowing fully to the smith. "Next time, drinks are on me. I owe you many a tale, especially this one if we survive it."

Dorgrin put a fist to his chest. "I'll pray ya do, all three of ya."

Yoder and Leeni waved to the big man before he turned back to his counter, then questioned The Wizard on their way out from under the tent fervently. The Wizard waved them off with his cane.

"All will be revealed when required, for now…. let's get you some fresh attire." He replied, hurrying ahead to outrun their questions. Leeni and Yoder frowned at each other but followed along.

Chapter Five:
I look amazing!

As the three rounded the spiraling sequence of stalls and shops that made up the Midnight Bazaar, Yoder became more and more suspicious of The Wizard. Leeni's whispering in his ear did not help either. She questioned why he hurried them off, questioned why he wouldn't answer their questions and even questioned the questions that they were hoping to get answers for. It was so dizzying that Yoder tuned her out completely and began to look at the wares on display all around them instead. Metalworks, jewelcrafts, woodcarvings, leathers and silks, cutlery, stone artifacts, and everything one never knew they could need crowded his vision. Just as it all became suddenly overwhelming, The Wizard called back to them as he veered off to lift the flap of an enclosed tent and duck inside.

Yoder and Leeni followed, Perrixstar shaking out its wings on Yoder's head. The young man reached the flap and pulled it back, moving to step inside when Leeni bumped against him. He looked at her, she looked at him and he mumbled an apology before ducking his head and stepping through first. Leeni huffed at the back of his head in frustration and stepped forward on his heels only to have the tent flap flop onto her head when Yoder let it go. Another frustrated sound left her lips, shoving the flap away to finally enter the enclosure while fingers brushed out her hair in an effort to compose herself.

The two found The Wizard already in conversation with a swarthy, dark-skinned man clad in fine robes of shimmering, colored fabric that reminded Yoder of Perrixstar's scales. The man sported a well-trimmed beard of black hairs that made his strong, proud facial features even more impressive somehow. Amidst the folds of layered robes were glistening metals, necklaces and clasps holding each layer to the next and upon the man's fingers were silver rings, one for each digit. Yoder assumed correctly that this was Maltheus, confirmed by The Wizard's hasty introduction.

"Yoder Hals, Leeni Vex, this is Maltheus Okanoafi." The Wizard said curtly, though the Clothier bent at the waist in a formal and graceful bow.

"Welcome, children," he said in a richly toned voice with an accent both different and somehow better than the way the others spoke. Leeni blushed slightly, finding the exotic man attractive in feature, fashion, and tone.

Yoder waved awkwardly. "Hi," he replied, then thought he might try to emulate the elegant man and attempt to bow. It was stiff and uncomfortable with his belly in the way, but Maltheus seemed to appreciate the gesture when Yoder stood up straight again. Rows of bright white teeth appeared when the outfitter smiled wide, a stark contrast to the night hue of his face.

The Wizard chuckled softly. "Right then. Maltheus shall take care of you for now, I've business to conduct. Stay put, both of you." he said firmly, pointing from one to the other with the crystal tip of his cane. "No wandering off this time. The bazaar has strict rules of conduct and even more strict punishments. Wouldn't want you losing a finger before we even set out." Yoder went white, swallowing and looking at Leeni who seemed unconcerned.

Maltheus only laughed, a deep, rumbling, but warm sound. "It has been many full cycles since anyone has lost a finger or hand. He is winding you up." The Wizard winked at Maltheus. "Take good care of them, within the agreed upon budget. My thanks." He said before hurrying out of the tent.

Yoder and Leeni awkwardly glanced at each other then all around them, the tented space was full of wooden racks where garments and armor were either displayed or stored on strings and strange, wooden triangles. Leeni tried not to gasp at the left corner, where Maltheus hung the most beautiful dresses she had ever seen. Long, elegant gowns with lace trim, soft wool pleats embroidered with flowers in golden thread. Maltheus noticed though, ever the sly and wise merchant.

"Come, girl. Come, there is plenty of time to indulge yourself. A woman is most beautiful when she is dressed in what she finds most beautiful, yes? Confidence is key."

Leeni's pale cheeks turned apple red. "I... I couldn't. I'd never afford anything so pretty. We're here for armor." Yoder nodded firmly, already eyeing a suit of glittering plate armor in the back of the tent.

"Go on." Maltheus encouraged, waving his black hands toward the dresses once more. "Those white curtains there, they are for privacy. Within, you will find a mirror. Try them on. Go on, pretty girl." He smiled wide and Leeni's cheeks felt like they might burst into flames.

"Oh my god, thank you!" She almost cried out, rushing to the rack to pull three from before she disappeared behind the white curtain.

Yoder rolled his eyes, not understanding the girl one bit. "I need armor. I'm a hero," he said haughtily. Maltheus turned with a swish of loose fabrics, clasping his hands together. "So, I hear. The Wizard says that you wish to not die completing your hallowed journey and so I shall help you find just what you need."

Yoder grinned. "I found it already," he said eagerly, walking over to the suit of plate mail he had set his sights on. He lifted his hand and patted the shoulder plate. "This is exactly what I was looking for."

Maltheus chuckled, approaching with casual, easy steps. "As you wish, young hero. Let us strap you in." Yoder smiled like a child on Christmas, untying his cloak, his pack, and his sword belt to set each down.

While Maltheus aided Yoder in donning the suit of armor, Leeni spent her time behind the curtain putting dress after dress on. She swayed before the mirror, posed this way and that way, even lifted the skirts to look at her rear's reflection. She smiled, she danced, and truly enjoyed herself. When she had finished with all three, the girl stepped out of the curtain in her clothes to put the dresses back and found Yoder grunting and groaning as Maltheus tried to stuff his fat body into a suit of full plate mail. Each time the outfitter pulled on a leather strap to conform a plate; Yoder winced.

Leeni crossed her arms over her chest and cocked her right hip out as she watched. "You look like a water skin caught in a wagon wheel."

Yoder glared at her. "Shut up! I can fi-it!" He hiccupped as Maltheus pulled hard and the chest plate dug into his gut. It hurt so bad. "I look amazing!" He called out, but both the girl and the clothier could hear the lie in his tone.

"You look fat," Leeni replied dismissively.

Perrixstar didn't enjoy being jostled, but it understood its mount's need for protection. He didn't have scales, after all, so he was buying some in order to emulate his master. The dragon took that as a compliment and only took exception when Maltheus attempted to put a large metal dome overtop of Perrixstar. It hissed at the clothier, who decided not to try again.

"Walk around, feel it out," Maltheus instructed Yoder, who waddled more than walked as the shin guards and straps made it difficult to bend his knees. He made it all of four waddled steps before the armor weighed him down. A fifth step took great effort and his attempt at a sixth ended in failure.

"I... can't move," Yoder mumbled. Leeni laughed hysterically at her companion, trapped in a suit of armor. The boy felt tears forming in his eyes. "Stop laughing at me!" He cried, shutting the girl up. Leeni looked down, remembering how she had cried when they met in the tavern. "Sorry..."

Maltheus moved to Yoder's aid, unbuckling the plate straps. "So, you see, young hero. Armor does not make a man great. Sometimes, it slows him down. It weighs heavier than a great man's duty even." As the chest plate loosened, Yoder exhaled heavily and instantly felt relief.

"Yeah…. I guess you're right." His dream of being a shining knight was crushed, he felt sick from the constraint of the metal and the embarrassment. Maltheus only smiled and continued speaking while Leeni picked out a few more dresses and disappeared behind the curtain again to play.

"A man's armor protects his skin, that is all. It is his actions, his honor, that makes him strong and respected." The outfitter suggested as he replaced each plate back upon the display rack. Yoder sighed, too sad to participate until Maltheus put a hand on his shoulder. "Come, I know just what you need."

When Leeni stepped out from the dressing curtain the second time, quite full of herself after realizing that she looked gorgeous in gorgeous dresses, she looked around the tent for Yoder and the clothier only to let out a gasp. Yoder stood to the far right, wearing a black chainmail tunic with bronze chain outline around the neck and sleeves, brown leather trousers with reinforced bronzed knee-plates and a hard leather breastplate fastened to his shoulders and around his sides. The armor did not push in on his gut, merely draped over it. He even looked thinner somehow about the middle.

"Whoa." Leeni said, blinking. Yoder looked at the sound, noticed the girl staring at him and blushed furiously. Maltheus billowed out Yoder's cloak and tied it back around his neck loosely then straightened the hood behind his neck for him.

"There, but a hero needs one last thing, I think." The outfitter admitted, walking away toward a rack of shields.

Leeni walked closer, looking Yoder over from head to toe. "You almost don't look fat." She said gently, but Yoder didn't know how to take a compliment, much less positive attention from the girl so he just stared at her with wide, frightened blue eyes.

"Dark colors are slimming to the eye," Maltheus explained, looking back from the rack of shields.

Yoder looked toward him, and his eyes shifted focus beyond. He walked past Leeni who opened her mouth to speak but closed it with a frown at being ignored. Yoder approached the rack of shields and lifted a round, wooden one off the rack. It was lacquered dark, circular in shape and fitted with a ring of blackened steel around its perimeter, but the center of the shield was painted with a large wolf's head, its dark eyes staring right back at Yoder's.

"This one," the boy said under his breath.

Maltheus smiled, nodding. "Very well. Oak wood, blackened steel. Very sturdy. It will protect you."

Yoder stared back at the painted gaze of the wolf, feeling something deep inside him connected to the image. Maltheus turned gracefully on Leeni.

"And now, pretty girl. It is your turn. Have you picked a dress that makes you feel beautiful?"

Leeni balked, blushing beet red and threw her hands up in front of her. "No! I'm not here for a dress. I need armor. I'm an adventurer!"

Maltheus laughed. "Can you not be an adventurer and wear a dress if you want to?"

Leeni frowned. She looked down, then up, then down again and finally up at the outfitter with great confusion. "...Can I?"

Maltheus chuckled softly. "Can you?" he asked in reply. "Come. Come! Show me your favorite," he instructed, shooing the girl away from Yoder and his shield. Perrixstar peered down at the wolf face, wondering what it's mount found so fascinating. Leeni returned to the rack and withdrew the wool pleat with flower embroidery and showed it to Maltheus. It was green like her tunic, and she liked how soft and warm it was on her skin.

Maltheus tilted his head. "I see. It is yours with my humblest regards."

Leeni's smile rose brilliantly. "Really?" She didn't know what to say.

Maltheus smiled. "Do not wear it in rain, wool is very constricting when wet. Now, for travel and danger. I think...leathers." He beckoned her to follow him, moving to another rack. "Your tunic is fine; I suggest these leather culottes." Showing the girl a pair of brown leather leggings that flare out at her knees rather than set tight to her legs. "They will protect you, but not restrict your speed. I see your weapons, they are for mobility and swift strikes, yes?" Leeni nodded, amazed by the man's knowledge. She took the culottes with her dress and followed the clothier dutifully.

While the two spent their time in the outfitter's tent, The Wizard had hurried off. He passed between two tent stalls to the outer rim of the cavern and with a quick glance about to make sure he wasn't being followed, hustled into a small tunnel further into the Nightrunners complex. Reaching the end, he spoke a special passcode "Interioris" to two men guarding a wooden door. One affirmed the code and unlocked the door for him. The Wizard stepped inside and withdrew his hat from his head. The room was dark and empty, a single candle in a stand sat on a single, small, wooden table. It was unlit. The Wizard waved his cane at it.

"Igni," he said, the wick of the candle suddenly bursting with small, blue flame. The Wizard knelt down before it, the candle's smoke wisped upward and began to gather into a cloud above it.

As the cloud formed thicker and thicker, the roiling surface of black and grey shimmered into the image of a dark-skinned man similar to Maltheus. His cheeks bore lines of black dots and his chin wore a long, straight, dark goatee.

"Report." The man said, to which The Wizard replied. "Merry meet, Reisland. Archmagus of the Seven."

Reisland's brown eyes narrowed. "What do you want?" He asked in the same tone a father might when their son or daughter suddenly offered to help and were being suspiciously kind about it.

The Wizard smiled. "All goes according to prophecy as I knew it would, an expense will be coming to the council from the Nightrunners for provisions."

Reisland pursed his lips. "Your fascination with that thief's guild is costly, farwalker. What is it for this time?"

The Wizard shrugged. "Arms and armor for two. The hero and one companion. A wagon, food, water, et cetera."

Reisland glowered in the smoke cloud. "All approved except the wagon."

The Wizard sat up, frowning. "We travel through Kurn! On foot, it will take well past a fortnight!"

Reisland the Elder harrumphed. "Find horses then. Travel light. It is safer and easier through Kurn than a wagon." The Wizard scoffed.

"I knew you were going to do this; you always make my job ten times more difficult. I just need a wagon and we'll have the fate of humanity saved in five days."

Reisland's brown eyes widened in anger. "I'm the council elder now! Not you! I have made my decision!" The archmage's face loomed in the smoke, glaring like an affronted God.

"It's your turn, that's all." The Wizard muttered indignantly. "When Alianore comes up, he'll let me have a wagon." Reisland made a guttural, frustrated sound, his visage disappearing from the smoke cloud that instantly began to dissipate.

The Wizard rolled his eyes, blew out the candle and rose to his feet in the dark. "That went well." He said to himself, affixing his cap back on his head. He walked back to the door and opened it, taking a step across the threshold with his cane in hand and stopped to stand between the two guardsmen. "So... Stables, it is." He smiled from one to the other and strolled away back down the tunnel to pass through the bazaar and out into town once more.

Nearly a full bell later, when horses and lodgings for the rest of the night were bought and paid for out of The Wizard's own coffers nestled deep in the magical expanse of his trouser pocket; he returned to Maltheus' Fittings and pushed through the flap once more. There waited Yoder in his new chainmail and leathers, backpack fastened under his cloak and wolf's head shield affixed to his left arm for he assumed that he would need it there if he were going to swing his sword with his right.

Leeni was leaned against Maltheus' worktable wearing her new brown leather culottes, leather boots with plated shin guards strapped around her calves, her green tunic with a hard leather jacket overtop to protect her body and her cloak overtop a backpack now too which housed her other pants and the wool dress Maltheus had gifted her. Leeni smiled.

"Welcome to Maltheus' Fittings, where you may always find what you see-Oh. It's you." Yoder grinned, so did Maltheus. The Wizard snorted.

"That any way to treat your benefactor. Look at you two! Proper adventurers now, eh?"

Yoder smiled at Maltheus. "Thank you, sir. For everything." He bowed again to the resplendent man, this time with far less awkwardness.

Maltheus returned the bow and smiled. "Walk in the light of God, young hero."

Leeni all but ran around the table and threw her arms around the clothier. "Thank you. Thank you." she said, bittersweet.

Maltheus closed his silk-swaddled arms around the small girl and hugged her back. "Be safe, pretty girl. Fight well, live strong." When Leeni let go and moved to join Yoder and the Wizard, Maltheus followed.

"And you, my old friend." The outfitter said to the foppish mage, lifting a hand to reach out and grasp the back of The Wizard's head. The Wizard smiled softly, doing the same with his opposing hand. The two men pressed forehead to forehead, and both spoke as one.

"Forever, guard the way. Forever. Viam Scire, My Brother."

Yoder and Leeni exchanged looks, unsure of the display. When the two men released each other, Yoder pointed from one to the other and finally settled on Maltheus. "Are you a wizard too?"

Maltheus chuckled. "I am a mage of the Mirrored Circle, yes."

The Wizard straightened his fine felt hat. "And my good friend growing up. We had the same archmage as our mentor." The two men exchanged nods then The Wizard beckoned for Yoder and Leeni. "Come along, we must return to Dorgrin's and collect Yoder's blade then settle in for the night."

Yoder moved to follow. "I'm hungry." He said.

"You're always hungry." The Wizard replied. "We'll get some food on the way." Leeni spared one last look at Maltheus, smiling softly at the merchant and mage who held up his hand to wave goodbye before she slipped out of the tent and followed the others.

Chapter Six:
That's not good...

Armor was heavy, Yoder had learned from his time in the outfitter's tent of the Midnight Bazaar, but this revelation was reinforced by the walk to the inn of Galarion's Hollow. By the time the trio reached the inn after Dorgrin's Forge, stood at the counter and made their orders, then climbed all the stairs up to their given room; Yoder was exhausted. So exhausted in fact that he had stripped off the armor immediately and sat at the small table when a maid brought their meal to eat quietly. Both the Wizard and Leeni saw this as suspicious behavior until they saw the weariness in the boy's eyes whose lids kept trying to close.

At one point, Leeni had to shoo Yoder to bed while she and the Wizard talked about the plan going forward for Yoder had begun to put meats and cheeses and fruit into his mouth on autopilot. He dreamed of a dragon eating all the sheep in his dream-farm's field. His eyes were closed, his breathing bordered on gentle snores as he picked a slice and pushed it through his lips.

When the sun woke Yoder the next day, he was wrapped up in a warm wool blanket on one of the two beds available in the room. He rolled over, scratched himself front and back then opened his eyes as he began to hear sounds. Sitting up, the boy found both Leeni and the Wizard already packing.

"Hurry up, sleepy." Leeni chided him with a smile. "It's almost time to go."

Yoder yawned wide, stretched his limbs as far as he could and rolled off the bed to don his clothes and armor again. Perrixstar fluttered its wings from the headboard of the bed to Yoder's head, nestling back on his head. Yoder smiled, finding the small dragon's presence an odd comfort now rather than an annoyance.

A full bell's toll later, Yoder stood on the road outside and above Galarion's Hollow with the reins of a dappled mare in one hand and his shield in the other. The Wizard sat atop a gray stud, brushing its mane gently while Leeni cooed to a smaller chestnut colored pony she was astride. The Wizard looked down at Yoder while steadying his mount.

"Up you go, my boy." He encouraged him. "We've a full day's ride to the border of Kurn and far further still."

Yoder, who had been very quiet all morning as the gravity of the quest fully settled upon him, offered a solemn nod and turned to climb onto the saddle of his mare. The weight of the armor, however, made a rote task quite difficult but after the third huffing push and a most embarrassing flounder on his belly over the saddle; managed to finally get himself seated on the dappled mare and off they went.

Halziyon's landscape was lush and verdant, green as green could be only speckled with rich brown tree trunks or sun-bleached stones. Yoder enjoyed the quiet calm of the ride, the horses clip-clopping musically upon the dusty road. The Wizard voiced concern over the state of the horizon, where gray and heavy clouds gathered. Leeni, however, was occupied with the odd silence of their hero. She spurred her pony to canter alongside Yoder's dappled mare.

"You alright?" The girl asked gently. Yoder glanced at her, watched her locks bounce about her pretty face and finally smiled as best he could.

"Yeah. I'm scared, you know? I've never left my village, much less Halziyon itself." The boy admitted, his rumbling gut bobbing under his breastplate. "Besides that, what if I fail? The whole world is doomed.

That's big, you know? Really…. big." His old friend Fear came for a visit, making Yoder sick to his stomach.

"Yeah…." Leeni replied, looking down at her hands holding her pony's reins then up at the dark sky ahead. "But don't worry, The Wizard's here with you. Right? Me too. We'll see this thing through, whatever it is."

Yoder sighed. "That's the thing. I don't know what's going to happen. He won't tell me what I'm supposed to do."

Leeni smiled, shrugging her slight shoulders. "Do you want him to? I mean, do you want to know exactly what fresh hell is waiting for you in The Teeth? When I ran with my…." Leeni trailed off, changed her words and started again. "When I was with those adventurers, they took jobs all the time. They had little information on what they'd face, but they faced it all the same. Sometimes, they got hurt. Real bad too, but they kept doing it. I started to admire that. Nothing stopped them, not fear, not danger. You can call it stupid if you want to, but I think it's courage. I think you're being courageous doing this, especially since it's you."

Yoder frowned at her. "What's that supposed to mean?" he asked, tense. His mare whinnied, sensing the rider's dismay.

Leeni giggled. "You're not an adventurer, Yoder. You're…." She tried to pick her words carefully, but Perrixstar atop Yoder's head finished her sentence.

"Fat." The Faerie Dragon purred. "And you're lazy. You complain about everything." The beast continued while Leeni gave Yoder a compassionate look but did not deny the criticism. Yoder felt ashamed, felt the tears begin to burn in his eyes again. He knew he was fat and lazy; he knew he wasn't the hero he wanted to be.

"And you're stupid. I love it." Perrixstar finished with laughter like wind chimes. "That's why I chose you as my slave."

Yoder's chubby face twisted in confusion. "How's that work?" He asked. Leeni giggled.

"Fat slave is kind because he's fat and lazy and stupid." Perrixstar purred upon Yoder's head. "Fat slave understands, even though he complains."

Leeni nodded. "You were kind to me after the tavern, you didn't have to be. You and the Wizard could've gone on with your quest and left me in the alley, but you came out to check on me. Even searched for me." She smiled softly, lifting a hand from her reins to reach out to the boy. Yoder was confused, he felt like he was being picked on, but they were also cheering him on all the same.

Perrixstar purred again. "Fat slave, you are scared but you keep going. Do not be afraid, your master will keep you safe." Yoder laughed, rolling his eyes then he saw Leeni's offered hand and his eyebrows raised. He reached out slowly, tentatively, to wrap his thick fingers around her smaller ones and instantly replaced his dream damsel with Leeni in his mind. Yoder smiled, squeezing her hand gently and Leeni squeezed back.

"We'll need to make camp!" called the Wizard. "Storm's coming." He pointed off the road to a thick copse of trees ahead. "There! Lash our tents to the trees so they don't blow away. Come!" He beckoned, heels tapping at the stud's middle to cue it to gallop forward.

Yoder and Leeni both did the same, speeding up the road to the trees indicated. Each dismounted, tied off their horses to one tree then hastily set about setting up camp after the Wizard unloaded a mid-sized tent pack from his magical pocket. With all the hustling, Perrixstar flapped its wings and lifted off Yoder's head to settle itself in the branches above.

The air grew colder by lunchtime, but the rain clouds were still further out and seemed to slow with their roiling heaviness. The Wizard watched lightning flash within the murky depths, frowning while the three ate leftover salted meats and bread from the night before in Galarion's Hollow.

"Might be hours before the storm reaches us," he said to the two, while Perrixstar glided down to roost on Yoder's head once again and be fed. Yoder did this without question, holding bits of meat up for the little dragon to burn with its tiny gout of dragon's fire then chomp down on. The Wizard swallowed a bit of salted meat, speaking up once more. "You two should spar, get some practice with your weapons." Yoder and Leeni looked at each other. Leeni nodded.

"It's a good idea, since we're here. I can show you some stuff," she said to Yoder, who blushed and smiled.

"Sure," he mumbled with a mouth full of bread.

Half a bell later, Leeni instructed Yoder on the basics of fighting "sword and board"; that is to say with sword and shield. The Wizard puffed on his ornate pipe and settled against a tree to watch. Yoder was not a fast learner and Leeni grew impatient with him many times, devolving their effort to hone skills into a shouting match more than once. Perrixstar nestled itself on a branch above to watch as well, laughing in that twinkling chime way at the two small humans and their antics. The Wizard wondered about the prophecy, the merit of taking this incapable, young man into enigmatic danger and yet, it was far too late now to turn back.

As Leeni and Yoder began to trade slow blows, Yoder awkwardly learned that he had to firmly hold his shield, so it didn't get knocked out of his hand constantly; the storm loomed closer and closer as did their fates and The Wizard let out a smoke-laden sigh. Despite his constant whining, Yoder had grown in the two days they had spent together thus far. When Leeni's short sword slapped Yoder's blade aside, bounced back and swatted his shield away; The Wizard watched her threaten the boy with the dirk and another argument ensued. He chuckled to himself but had to admit that for all of Yoder's complaining, the boy never gave up.

The two youths sparred and argued for two whole bells before the rains finally came and all four companions retreated to the dry safety of the tent. Yoder whined about being sore, shedding his armor and flopping onto his bedroll to snack on the last of the salted meats and some fruit he had stashed in his pack. Leeni had more poise, relaxing on her own bedding beside Yoder's and critiquing his lack of combat prowess. The two argued, while Perrixstar gobbled up meat and The Wizard consulted his map of Kurn quietly.

So enthralled by his planning, The Wizard was unaware that silence had overtaken the tent. He rubbed his chin, deep in focused thought over the best way to navigate through the wastes that he could only be jarred from his thoughts by a loud smack. He looked up, found Yoder holding his cheek and Leeni glaring at him with great fury and redness about her face. Perrixstar laughed hysterically, rolling itself over and kicking its tiny, clawed legs about.

"You bastard!" Leeni bellowed, throwing her tiny self at the large boy who looked like he was fit to burst into tears. Yoder toppled backwards, the small girl on top of him and cried out for help as she slapped him not once nor twice. Three times, each hand batted at his head.

Yoder flailed, afraid to fight back. The Wizard blinked, confused and just watched as the scrappy, little Leeni grabbed the boy by the neckline of his tunic with one fist and cocked back the other. Yoder flapped his lips, trying to find words but the girl socked him in his right eye and made him sob uncontrollably before she crawled off him, grabbed her cloak and ran out of the tent into the storm.

"I'm sorry!" Yoder called out after her, reaching with one hand toward the fleeing girl's back while the other covered over his struck eye.

"What did you do?" The Wizard asked, aghast and more than a little perplexed.

Yoder sniffled, whining and sitting up fully. "I kissed her? I thought…. I mean…. we were…." The boy stumbled over his explanation, all his reasons for doing so now questioned silently after getting punched in the eye.

The Wizard winced. "That's not good…"

Perrixstar's laughter had not subsided, though the creature rolled itself back onto its feet. Yoder scowled, tears running down his jowls, at the dragon. The Wizard sighed.

"Boy, you have a lot to learn about women. Though, I admire your bravery." He said, rolling up his map.

"I thought she liked me!" he moaned, humiliated and in pain.

The Wizard chuckled. "Oh yeah, that bruised eye is definitely a sign of amorous intent."

Yoder scowled at him too. "But she held my hand and we trained together, she even said she'd stay with me. I thought…" The Wizard held up his hand to stop the lad there.

"What you thought doesn't matter, Yoder. Now that it's over, think about it. Should you try to kiss her again?"

Yoder looked down, dejected, and mumbled. "No."

"Good lad. Understand that I'm not going to tell you you're wrong. You had a feeling, you acted on that feeling. She has denied you. I suggest you consider that you have a friend in her and little more than that. Maybe, that will change but now the decision rests solely on her."

Yoder sobered, listening and gaining control of his breath. "I should apologize then." He announced, moving to rise but The Wizard once again held up his hand to stop him.

"Leave her be. If she returns, then be the man and apologize. Don't wait for her to speak to you. Admit your mistake, show her your respect and let her choose from there."

"But the storm? What if something happens to her out there?" Yoder asked, struggling with the sense that he had upset her and made her flee from him into danger.

"We all make choices, my boy. Good or bad, right or wrong. Remember?" The Wizard answered and Yoder nodded to him.

"Yeah. It's my fault though. I have to make sure she's safe," he added firmly, climbing up to his feet and pulling his cloak around his shoulders.

The Wizard watched, nodding in reply. "Do what your heart says is right."

Yoder strapped on his sword, took up his shield and crossed the small tent to its fluttering flap. The wind howled, rain pattered hard on the heavy fabric outside and Yoder knew he was afraid. He hesitated only a moment, glancing over at the Wizard sitting in the opposite corner. "I have to."

He left The Wizard after taking a deep breath, pushing past the tent flap out into the heavy winds and beating rain. Perrixstar hopped toward the tent flap and sat on its haunches, waiting for Yoder's return while the boy outside pulled his hood up over his head and clutched it closed around his neck.

"LEENI!" He called out, but the wind bellowed right back and set his cloak fluttering away so the rain could soak his tunic and leathers. Yoder tried to pull the cloak around himself more with his shield hand while holding the shield still and this proved very difficult to do but somehow, the shield helped protect him from the wind as well. He started forward, reaching one of the trees.

"LEENI!" Yoder called out again, pushing himself past the tree to the next one. His head lifted, he thought he heard something and looked to the side then started that way.

Rain battered him, wind pushed him back, but Yoder refused to submit. She was out there somewhere, and it was all his fault. Leeni was stronger, braver than he was, but the storm terrified him, and he had to reason that she was at least a little scared. If she was a little scared, he couldn't leave her out here in the dark and the cold and the wind. Every step the boy took was hard, harder than wearing his armor and walking around. The gale resisted him at every turn, tried to shove him this way and that. Trees loomed in the dark, swaying and creaking ominously. He heard the noise again but couldn't locate it.

"LEENI! WHERE ARE YOU?!" he called out only to have his mouth filled with stifling, rushing wind and cold rain. Yoder spit the water out, ducking his head down some before he pushed onward once more.

He had no idea how far he'd gone into the storm searching for her when he heard a cry more clearly. "Help me!" He was sure of it.

"I'm coming! Keep yelling!" Yoder listened, scrunching his rain-streaked face in confusion when he heard what sounded like "Pound Beer" called out. However, he heard it all the same and it came from ahead, so he pressed on through the storm. "I'm coming! Hold on!" He bellowed, stumbling forward. Bumbling through muddy grass, Yoder put one boot in front of the other until his boot missed the earth somehow. With a strangled cry, he pitched forward and fell, tumbling end over end.

Yoder splashed into soft mud, it clung to his cloak and the boy flailed about to try to find his footing again.

"Oh, Great!" He heard Leeni's voice call to his left, so he pushed his muddy hood back to see her. Leeni was mere feet away, pressed against the wet, earthy wall. "Nice job, hero. Now we're both stuck!" she snapped, smacking the pooled mud up to her thighs. Yoder looked down, noting he too was leg-deep in muck. He looked up at the dirty, mud-caked girl and began to slosh his way toward her.

"I'm sorry!" he called.

Leeni bellowed back. "It's fine! We have to get out of here before this hole fills up!" She explained as loudly as she could against the wind's cry. Yoder reached her side, resting against the muddy wall.

"No. I mean, I'm sorry for kissing you!" he called out. "We wouldn't be in this mess if I hadn't, but I really had no right to do that in the first place. I thought you liked me and…."

Leeni yowled. "Is this really the time?! Really?!"

Yoder frowned, thought it through and shook his head. "No. You're right!"

He turned to the wall, attempted to climb it but only slipped on the loose earth which pulled free. "I can't get out! Here, let me try to push you up!" He suggested. "Lift your foot!" Yoder added, bending down to shove his free hand into the muck to search for her leg. He found it, felt along her calf to her foot and under. "Ready?!"

Leeni bellowed a resounding "Yes!"

Yoder pulled her foot up as high as it would go, the girl pushed against it while putting her hands on the top of his head. He grunted, she lifted and once one leg was free of the mud; she stepped up onto his shoulder. "OW!" Yoder groaned loudly in protest as Leeni lifted her other leg, standing on his shoulder then stepped up onto his head and finally pushed herself over the edge of semi-solid earth.

"I'm out!" she called, rolling herself around to lean as carefully as she could over the ledge. "Give me your hands!"

Yoder grabbed her hands, tried to dig his boots in the loose soil but it was so wet that he got one foot up while Leeni pulled with all her might only to lose his grip. She wasn't strong enough to lift him and the mud made everything so slippery. She tried one more time, screaming into the storm with all her might to pull the fat youth up toward her but his hands slipped free of hers and Yoder fell backward. His arms swung about as he splashed into the rising mud, sinking beneath its murky surface.

"YODER!" Leeni cried out, her mud-covered arms reaching as far and as hard as they could.

Leeni watched the mud pool with wide, horrified eyes but the large boy didn't surface. "YODER!!" she screamed, fingers clawing at the mud wall in frustrated desperation. The rains fell harder still, the hole filling faster and faster with muddy water as Leeni waited; lying there on the edge.

Chapter Seven:
It's all relative.

The first thing Yoder recognized when his mind returned to him was the squishy wetness. He blinked, his eyes stinging in their sockets, and he dragged his hands through the squishy wetness toward his face. Any attempt to clear his vision was only made worse by the clinging muck and there was no chance of cleaning them off as his clothing was saturated by the stuff. Every time he tried to plant his feet under him, lifting himself from the squelching morass to escape its clutches, they slipped from under him and left the boy scrambling.

Time felt like it crawled. He thought the soft, messy fluid mass would never end as he pushed himself up over and over, only to slip and fall back down again. More than once, he wanted to just lay there and let it end. There seemed like no escape, no way to see, no way to walk or crawl out of this disgusting prison.

And then, when all hope seemed utterly lost, a shaking hand reached out one last time and lay on the grass. Each tiny, firm plant under his hand was a thousand hopeful grasps. Land. Like a sailor lost at sea, Yoder cried out in exultant glee and dug his fingers into the firm soil. Not muck. The boy pulled himself forward again, reaching out with his other hand and patting about over the patch of grass he'd found. He began to laugh, his mouth tasted like mud, and the laughter was halted by a profound urge to vomit. So, he did, spewing up what remained of his last meal but never, ever letting go of the grass.

As he felt the muck give way to firm ground under his belly, Yoder rolled over onto his back and heaved for air through his gross mouth. His nose was stuffed, unable to carry air and it reminded him that he was covered in squishy, heavy detritus. His hands whipped furiously at the grass, feeling the clinging sludge break away and let go until he could wildly swipe at his face. Thick globs clung to his hands, so he swung them out until the gunk flicked off. He even stuck his fingers in his nostrils, carving out the muck that stoppered them until he could inhale again.

Sitting up finally, Yoder had cleared enough of the mud from his face to open his eyes and he looked about him in stunned confusion. Grassland, trees, brush behind him. Birds sang above like heavenly hosts. Ahead of him, a sprawling mudslide had crushed a swath through the forest, a thick, light brown blob that must have rolled for miles onward. He blinked a few times, squinting in the daylight. Day. It was daytime! How long had he been tossed about by the avalanche of sludge, he didn't know. All the boy knew was that he was alive.

Better kismet caught his eye. For while his sword was still attached to his hip somehow, his shield lay in the field of mud, caught on a protruding stone by its wrist strap. Yoder sighed, working tiredly to his feet before he began to wipe caked mud off himself. It clung hard and thick, layers and layers of wet dirt refused to let go of him. It took a very long time to free it all and when he realized the futility of trying to clean himself up completely, Yoder decided to carefully trudge back into the mudflow to retrieve his shield.

Being able to see made traversing the mud easier, not to mention the lack of panic aided him in keeping calm. Still, he had to put his booted feet down deep in the muck and pull them up slowly lest he'd lose one of those boots to the sucking miasma. It made the trek very slow. When he reached the shield though, Yoder bent down and slipped it off what he thought was a stone from far away. It wasn't.

Yoder wasn't sure what it was, really. The boy crouched down with furrowed brows and tilted his dirty head. The object his shield had caught on was metal. Not unrefined metal, forged metal. It was obvious, smoothed and shaped to a point. He reached out with his other hand, while the right tucked the shield under his armpit. Fingers curled around the sloping cylindrical shape, and he gave it a pull. It didn't come free of the mud, but it moved easily and the suddenness of how easy it was made Yoder yank his hand back like it might bite him.

He stared at the cylinder, small, maybe as thick as a sword-hilt and now bent to the right slightly. Maybe it was some broken weapon stuck fast in the mud. He reached for it again, wrapped his fingers around it and pulled in the other direction. The cylinder bent back to its original place but wouldn't budge further than that. He let go, his fingers beginning to wipe away the mud around it as best he could until the base of the object was revealed to the light. A wheel of some kind, very small like the cylinder, attached to a base deeper in the sludge perhaps. Yoder felt over the contours, noting that the circle allowed the cylinder to bend down but not up. How strange. Like a child, he began to bend and straighten the cylinder over and over again while he inspected it. That is, until the ground began to heave.

Yoder screamed, not that anyone was around to laugh at the girlish cry. He fell back on his butt in the mud, but soon turned round and scrambled with muck-flinging limbs back toward the grass outside of the mud-field again. A terrible, unearthly groan erupted from the mud behind him, spurring the boy to flee faster. He launched himself onto the grass, rolling over onto his back to pull his shield out from under his arm in front of him. The groaning grew louder, joined by a demonic, low hum. Yoder was terrified, clamoring up onto his muddy feet to set his shield on his arm and then draw his muddy sword from its scabbard. He set himself like Leeni had taught him, shield arm raised, and blade laid upon the top of the shield with the tip pointed at the massive mound of mud rising in the field ahead.

The mud bubbled up and broke open, sludge dripped down a huge, round shape like a gigantic ball. The cylinder he'd played with had replicants, four of them and each one was attached to what looked like an enormous hand. That enormous hand was attached to a strange, bendy, thin tube that in turn attached to the gigantic ball that rose up from the morass. It lurched upward, rising higher and higher with Yoder's panic. He felt his armpits dripping sweat, his mouth going dry. It was some sort of monster, unearthed by the mudslide.

The monster loomed, mud dripping off of it as the gigantic ball turned toward him. The turn revealed a second tube ending in a second, enormous hand with four cylindrical fingers that made the mass seem vaguely humanoid. At the very apex of the ball, it opened with a horrid screech. Mud flew everywhere as something popped up out of the top. A smaller ball with a plate like a crab shell on top. Yoder gulped, shrinking back further from the monster and the mud-field. Two blue lights popped on in the small ball under the crab-shell plate. They flashed on and off three times, Yoder nearly soiled his already soiled trousers. He was about to drop his sword and shield to run when sound boomed from the giant creature, echoing like a voice in a cavern.

"Quis Es?"

Once again, Yoder let out a high-pitched screech and did exactly as he intended. Sword fell, his shield was pushed off his arm and the large, muddy youth turned on a heel. He ran as hard as his fat legs would carry him, arms pumping up and down. The mud monster watched, lurching forward up out of the muck on two heavy weights attached to tubes like its arms. It extended those legs to fling one weight onto the grass and a grinding, cranking noise pulled its mass along the tube then retracted the other leg in one, huge step onto solid land. It bent forward, looking down at the wolf's head shield and muddy sword. The blue lights flashed, growing wider after as it reached down with its huge mitt and fingers to clutch both in its grasp.

As Yoder fled through the trees, tripping on roots and bouncing his bulk off tree trunks, the sound of heavy thumps continued to follow him and enhanced the terror that made him run to begin with. The boy was unfit though and the further he ran, the harder it was to breathe. Frantically, he threw himself around a large, standing stone and then scrambled to put his back against it. Chest heaving, his mind starting to go numb; Yoder struggled to regain his air as he hid behind the stone and listened to the heavy thumping growing louder and louder. There was another sound as well, a high-pitched call he recognized but his frightened mind could not reconcile.

"Slaaaaaaaay-yaaaaaaaaaave?!" Called Perrixstar, swooping effortlessly between the branches of trees as it soared about in search of Yoder. It wasn't all that concerned; slaves could be replaced. This one was fun and all, so it would be sad for a minute if its fat slave was truly lost but in the end; it'd be fine. Shimmering wings unfolded and flapped wide, hoisting the serpent-like neck and small body aloft. "Slaaaaaaaave? Where did you goooooooo?" It sang loudly, like playing a game of hide and seek.

Yoder's senses latched onto the sound, his heart skipping a beat. "I'm here! Oh, God. I'm here!!" He cried out without thinking. Perrixstar giggled and arced its way down to swoop onto Yoder's head but found him all dirty and diverted course. It flipped itself in mid-air, doing a loop to come up fluttering its wings and face to tiny dragon face with its slave.

"I found you! That was fun. Why are you dirty? Go wash your head, fat slave."

•

Yoder was so happy to see the little dragon that he didn't even scowl, he did wave his hands in front of it though. "Shhhh!! There's a monster after me!" He warned the dragon, whose head twisted sideways like it didn't understand.

"Is this another game?! Yay!"

The thumping began to echo, much closer now. Yoder almost burst into tears at the misunderstanding between him and the faerie dragon. "No! Wait, yes. It's a game. Go get Leeni and the Wizard so they can play too. Hurry!" He said in a hushed tone.

Perrixstar squinted its little, glowing, snake eyes, it almost seemed skeptical. "Okay!" It said suddenly and with a hard flap of its beautiful wings, took off up into the air again to fly away.

Yoder huddled against the stone after Perrixstar had gone, going as quiet and still as he could. The thumping was all around him now as the muck-monster loomed on the other side of the stone, sword and shield gripped in its left, huge hand.

"Ubi Es?" It echoed out, the sound deep and threatening. Yoder clasped his hands over his face to muffle his panicked breathing or any accidental shrieks he might let out.

And shriek, he did. One of the creature's large, round, weights soared overhead and thumped into the grass mere feet ahead of him. The grindy, cranking sound pulled the gigantic ball across the sky above him and Yoder couldn't stop himself. The cranking sound pulled the other round weight toward its base, but the weight crashed into the standing stone Yoder had hidden behind. It shuddered and the boy rushed away from it, afraid it would fall.

"Don't kill me! Please!" he cried out, slamming himself into a tree trunk nearby to flatten his back against it.

The muddy weights firmly set in the ground, crushing the grass beneath them, the giant ball twisted toward the running human and then hovered forward some. Its blue lights flashed once under the crab-shell plate. Those lights aimed at the terrified boy, but it extended its left hand out toward Yoder and the fist turned. Yoder squeaked, but rather than get pounded into dust; he watched the fingers open up to reveal his sword and shield.

"Haec Mittis." The giant thing echoed firmly. Yoder blinked up at it, unsure what to do. The muddy monster inched its hand closer to him. "Eas Capere." It echoed from its mass.

Yoder didn't understand it, but the gesture seemed to be offering the weapons, so he slowly took each from the flat, metal plate that made up the monster's palm. He slid his sword into its scabbard carefully, then took the shield in hand. The muck covered thing withdrew its huge hand with grinding cranks then turned the palm upward. It swung back and forth like it was waving gently.

"Salve, Vir." It echoed.

Yoder lifted his head, inhaling and exhaling rapidly still from fright. "I... uh...I don't understand your words," he explained in a stammering tone.

The creatures' two eyes, the blue lights that Yoder reasoned must be eyes, contracted into pinpoints for a moment before they widened back out again. Its central mass, the big ball, shuddered. Wisps of smoke trailed up through the hole where Yoder reasoned its head had come out of.

"Lowland Speech Recognized. Translating. Hello, Man." It echoed out in words Yoder could understand. Yoder's mouth fell open. He stared, wide-eyed, at the tall thing looming over him. It was half as tall as the tree he was pressed against and round as a boulder in the middle.

"Uh. H-hello," he replied in awe, waving weakly with one hand.

"Who are you?" The muddy monster echoed, though Yoder wasn't sure he could call it a monster anymore. It wasn't trying to hurt him and the mud that slid off its spherical middle revealed what looked like dull brass in the sunlight beaming down between the trees. He wasn't certain he could quantify this creature in any terms he knew.

"My name is Yoder." The boy replied, putting a hand on his chest. "Yoder." It, whatever it was, mirrored the motion by slowly turning its own large hand to set on the metal ball that was its body.

"Y. Six. Six. R." Its voice echoed. Yoder blinked, tilting his head as he stared up at the gigantic...thing. Just like him, a name beginning and ending in the same letters. That would be confusing.

"Can I call you Sixer?" he asked curiously.

The blue lights that Yoder now determined were its eyes contracted and returned to normal size again. "Affirmative." It replied tinnily.

"What's that mean?" Yoder asked, clearly undereducated.

"It means Yes." The giant replied.

"Why didn't you just say that then?" Yoder questioned more boldly; he'd seen so many strange things in the last two days now that he had unconsciously begun to grow a spine. At least, he found it after knowing he wasn't going to die screaming anyways. The brass giant didn't move, not a twitch. He started to wonder if it had fallen asleep or something, save that the blue lights were still on in what Yoder assumed was its face.

"Hello?" he asked, slightly worried his forwardness had doomed him.

It echoed suddenly. "I do not know. It is all relative."

Yoder sighed out a breath he'd been holding in the silence, sinking back against the tree with a tense laugh. "It's all relative? What does that mean?"

The giant's center began to crank, its leg tubes retracting into itself to lower down closer to the weights that Yoder reasoned were its feet. Was it crouching? Sitting down? Yoder was amazed at how human it behaved. The giant echoed out its explanation.

"To my assembly line, affirmative is the correct response. To you, man, Yes is the correct response. Affirmative means Yes, they are two words with the same definition." Yoder's features squeezed together, his brows furrowed, and his lips pursed. That made sense.

"It's all relative…" Yoder repeated softly, committing the phrase to memory.

The brass giant shrank its leg tubes till they disappeared completely, the sphere of its central mass resting directly on the two heavy weights that were definitely its feet. Yoder stared at it for a moment, gathering courage. It had been understanding so far, answered his questions and not pounded him into a sticky mush. He raised his chin, trying to show less fear.

"What are you, Sixer? I've never seen anything like you before." He hadn't seen much of anything except humans and fields, but that didn't seem relevant at the time.

Sixer hummed from its core, echoing an answer. "I am a service drone of the city state of Solaria, my primary function is maintenance and upkeep of the energy ministry."

Yoder stared in blank awe; everyone knew the legends of Solaria. Only found in stories passed around these days, Solaria was a fairytale. Nothing more, but this thing before him claimed to be from there. It boggled the boy's mind.

"Solaria? That's impossible. Solaria isn't real." he said, but his tone sincerely didn't believe his words.

Sixer's blue lights flashed. "Solaria is real. My assembly series is designed to build, repair, and fuel the energy department to ensure optimal function of the city's processes for the betterment of all."

"No way...." Yoder whispered, curiosity and joy overriding his fears. If this creature was to be believed, and it seemed incapable of lies; then the legends were true and somewhere out there was a shining, magical city of absolute perfection. "How did you get stuck in the mud then? Is Solaria nearby?" He inquired eagerly, wondering if he would be the first man to lay eyes on the fabled kingdom for real.

Sixer hummed, responding. "Negative. Solaria is located two hundred miles north." Yoder frowned, once again not understanding.

"Negative? Miles? What are those?"

Sixer echoed explanations. "Negative is our term for an incorrect assessment, it means No. A mile is a unit of measuring distance Solarians use to calculate destinations and lengths of regions in the Cartographic Guild." More words Yoder didn't grasp, but the explanations were enlightening. Negative meant No, miles were a way to tell how far something was.

"Okay. So, if Solaria is that far away, how did you get stuck in the mud with me?"

The brass giant hummed again, filling the lack of answer with ambient sound until it was ready to do so. "There was a cataclysmic event, my sequence of assembly and I were excavating fuel ore, the world broke around us. I was damaged in a fall. That is all I recall in my data stores before I became aware of something pulling my finger. When I rebooted, I found you, man."

Yoder chuckled. He liked being called man, but it was strange as well, not friendly. "Yoder. I am a man, but you can use my name." He advised the giant. "And…. That was me, pulling your finger. I didn't know what you were."

Sixer hummed for a brief moment, its blue lights shrinking to smaller circles in its blank head sphere. "Then you are the catalyst of my reboot. Thank you for waking me, Yoder."

Yoder beamed proudly, lifting his muddy head just a little higher. "You're welcome, Sixer."

Chapter Eight:
You've got to be kidding!

By the time Leeni reached the camp through the harrowing storm that beat the trees and earth with heavy rain, The Wizard had been dozing off sitting up with his pipe burnt out and precariously hanging from his lips. Perrixstar was fast asleep, similar to the Wizard, with a small sliver of meat dangling from its tiny maw. Both were startled when Leeni burst through the tent flap, blinked at them and jumped back out of the tent to look around at the dry grass under her feet. She looked up, her hair matted to her face and her clothes absolutely soaked and muddy to watch the rain disappear a few feet above her head. The wind didn't even threaten the tent, it and its occupants were completely safe within what appeared to be a sphere of perfectly calm weather.

So confused and awed by this, she almost forgot what she had rushed back to say. When the urgency returned, she shoved her head through the flap. "Yoder!" The girl cried out. Perrixstar, bristling its scales in annoyance, perked up its head on its long neck at mention of its slave's name. "He fell! I couldn't pull him up! Hurry!" She explained with rushed breaths and frantic eyes.

The Wizard dashed off the floor, dropping his pipe. "Show me," he said firmly, all but walking through the girl to get out of the tent. Leeni backed up quickly, her muddy boots slipping in the dry grass. Perrixstar soared from the tent, hot on The Wizard's heels but it was waved off by the man. "The storm winds are too strong for you, little one. Remain. We will find him." The Wizard commanded, withdrawing his felt hat from his coat pocket and securing it over his hair.

Perrixstar hissed, swooping around to land on the dry grass at the foot of the tent flap. "If my fat slave dies, you will be responsible."

The Wizard inhaled a steely breath. "If he dies, we're all done for."

The Wizard followed Leeni into the storm which battered them soundly as soon as they left the area of calm. He raised an arm to shield his eyes and trudged forward as fast as he could to keep up with the girl's fearful scramble. Through the howling winds and pelting rain, they struggled until Leeni brought him to the edge of a sprawling mudslide that roiled across the forest floor like a vast river of rich brown sludge. The two searched for hours before giving up and returning as carefully as they could to the tent and its safe zone.

Muddy and soaked, Leeni shivered from the cold and collapsed on the grass in stunned silence. The Wizard coughed once, shook out his coat and instantly dried.

Perrixstar hissed at the two humans who returned without the third that belonged to it. "Where is my fat slave?" It asked angrily, pacing back and forth in the dry grass like a fretting mother.

"We couldn't find him." Leeni said softly, aghast and afraid that the annoying, chubby brat who had saved her life might just have given his own to do it.

The Wizard cursed himself silently, lips pursed tight with guilt after the faerie dragon's question. He'd failed, doomed the whole world by letting the boy go off on his own like that.

Perrixstar flared its beautiful wings at them, coiling its long neck as if it were going to strike at them like a serpent. "I will go, retrieve my fat slave."

The Wizard sighed. "Wait until the rains stop, then we will resume the search. At the very least....to bring his body home to his mother." His tone dreading the unknown.

Leeni wiped her eyes and crawled into the tent to suffer in silence. The Wizard remained out in the patch of dry grass, watching for the storm to show any sign of passing by or letting up while Perrixstar glowered at his back.

And so it was that many bells later and more than a bell of Perrixstar's searching that the little dragon soared hastily on beating wings back to camp to tell the others. They packed up quickly, overjoyed, and rushed out to see their lost companion with their very own eyes. Leeni had changed into the dress she had received from Maltheus the outfitter to let her armor and garments dry while The Wizard never changed at all.

When the three reached the rock formation, neither could believe their eyes. A giant monstrosity, round like a ball rested in the copse of trees and at first, Leeni assumed it was some mythic edifice. There were stories of such things in the taverns she once frequented, but as she drew nearer and heard the voice, her confusion grew. Yoder's nasal voice was calm and friendly, chatting amiably with someone who bore an odd vocal cadence. It almost sounded like when she used to talk into her father's old helm as a child. Resonant.

"Yoder?!" She called out from the other side of the spherical edifice then screamed in horror when the top of it swung around like an owl and two blue lights narrowed in its empty round head. The Wizard stopped short, a look of stunned recognition on his angular face while

Perrixstar swooped around the giant's head and dove to land on Yoder's. It padded a circle then hissed. "Your head is still dirty, fat slave." It said, disgusted, but Yoder paid no mind. He was quickly waddling around Sixer.

"Leeni?!" He called back, ignoring the protests of the faerie dragon. "Oh my God, you're okay!" he cried out, appearing around Sixer's bulk covered in dried muck still but with the brightest smile he had ever smiled in his whole life. He threw his arms out wide as the pretty girl in the pretty dress rushed toward him, but his eyes widened as she skids to a stop and cocked back with her right fist. "Lee…" was all the boy got out before she punched him in the cheek.

Yoder spun, the world went dizzy and then upturned as he crashed to the ground. Perrixstar evacuated the ship, flapping off Yoder's head before he fell.

"You fat asshole!" he heard Leeni bellow, his cheek throbbed, and his eyes burned hot, but Yoder rolled over and sprawled out in the grass.

Sixer rolled toward him slightly, looming above with wide blue lights. "Yoder. Shall I deploy combat countermeasures to eliminate the female human threat?" the giant asked emotionlessly.

Yoder groaned, lifting a dirty hand to rub his face. "No. She's okay, she does that." He moaned.

"If you EVER do something so stupid like that again and don't die, I'll kill you myself!" Leeni snarled down at him, one fist on her hip and the other hand pointing with great accusation. "I can handle myself. I don't need you to save me, you jerk!" she added, accentuating her point by kicking him in the shin with her booted foot.

"OW!" Yoder cried, doubling over to grasp his leg with both hands.

Sixer's blue lights flashed off then on. It resonated a question. "Why is the female human hurting you, Yoder?"

Yoder opened his mouth to respond, but the fiery girl cut him off. "Because he's stupid and he deserves it!" She snapped, her pale face bright red as she whipped her wild hair and looked at the sphere. Instantly, she realized she was yelling at something that could crush her. The girl shrank back a step, fear gaining control of her outrage.

The Wizard watched all this, chuckling and he passed by Leeni calmly to offer his hand down to Yoder. "I thought we'd lost you, lad. I am full glad you're not dead." He said cheerily while Yoder pulled himself up off the grass with the offered hand's help.

"Really? You were worried about me? Thanks." Yoder replied, genuinely smiling. He didn't think The Wizard cared.

He was right. "Of course, my boy. If you die, the whole of the world is doomed." The Wizard explained carelessly, turning to inspect the giant sphere. Yoder looked crestfallen.

"Right. This is Sixer, I found him in the mud."

The giant peered down at the foppish man in the felt hat. "Hello. I am Sixer, model designation: Y-66R." It resonated from its core.

The Wizard smiled wide; his suspicions confirmed. "Ohh, aren't you a beauty. Worker drone, yeah? Solarian design. I've seen diagrams of you, you're fantastic."

Sixer stared, resonating a response. "Thank you, male human."

"Oh, I'm more than human, my friend. Look closer, look…. hard." The Wizard replied cheekily, his grin akin to a cat with a bowl of cream.

Sixer's blue lights narrowed, widened, narrowed again, then widened fully. "Apologies, Maker. My recognition systems are still being rebooted. How may I serve you?"

Yoder cast a surprised and all too familiar look of confusion between the giant and his guide. "Maker? Did you make him?" he asked, pointing a stubby finger at Sixer. Leeni drew closer, wondering what they were talking about while Perrixstar beat its wings for altitude to return to Yoder's head.

The Wizard didn't even look at his ward, enamored with the massive, muddy sphere. "Mmmmmno, but my ancestors did. The last council of Solaria, predating the Mirrored Circle by…. almost a hundred years now," he explained softly, distractedly.

"But Solaria is gone." The Wizard added suddenly, his grin replaced by a scowl. "Where'd you come from? It's been ages."

Yoder answered. "He said he and his brothers were digging up rocks for fuel or something and he fell, said something about his systems repairing."

Sixer confirmed with a resounding. "Correct." The Wizard's brows began to slowly lift. "Of course…. automatic repair. It must have been quite the fall to take this long to repair your processors." Sixer resonated, "Correct" in reply. The Wizard rubbed his chin for a moment, then spoke up again. "Y dash Six Six R…. Sixer." Adjusting with the use of the nickname Yoder employed. "You will escort us through the Razor Teeth of Levistrax," he commanded.

"Confirmed." Sixer replied tinnily.

"Can I wash this mud off and change and eat? I'm starving." Yoder requested, glancing at Leeni who huffed and looked away indignantly. He hung his head, defeated until The Wizard replied.

"Of course. Of course. I've some food in reserve. Here," he said, reaching into his pocket until half his arm disappeared into the depths. He withdrew a folded cloth of red and white squares, unfolding it with a flourish to lay the large cloth on the grass.

Next out of the magical pocket was a wicker basket with a loaf of bread, half a wheel of cheese, dried mutton wrapped in leaves, and apples. Yoder stared at the contents like he'd never seen food before, his stomach growling and his mouth ready to drool. The Wizard was not done though, drawing a water skin from the pocket next which he held out to Yoder, followed by the boy's backpack left in the tent last night.

"Go, wash up and put fresh clothes on. The skin won't empty, use as much as you need."

Yoder took both with relief, scampering around behind the large rock on the other side of Sixer. The Wizard sat down, pulling his pipe and tobacco so he could stuff and light the pipe up.

Leeni sat down quietly, breaking the bread into small chunks first and the cheese next. She didn't eat, just toiled in silence until the Wizard cleared his throat.

"He's fine." The man said softly.

Leeni snapped her angry eyes up at The Wizard, but they softened instantly. "I know that. He's still a jerk." She said without conviction.

The Wizard chuckled, puffing on his pipe. "He's our jerk now." Commented with a sly observing gaze at the girl.

Her face reddened, but she didn't look up from prying a cut of dried meat into bite sized portions. "Shut up." She mumbled.

Sixer watched the ritual of breaking bread in the grass curiously, its blue lights adjusting in size and shape as it focused on individual things and actions until the two fell to silence. Unbeknownst to them, it turned off its optical lights and began to diagnose itself through self-repair protocols in its central processing parameters.

When Yoder returned, he was clean and dressed in his spare blue tunic and brown trousers again. His armor and clothing were draped on the stone to dry in the sunshine while they ate. He waddled over to the two sitting on the cloth in the shade of Sixer's great bulk, lowering himself down and eagerly reaching for a piece of bread. Leeni picked it up first, transferring it to Yoder's hand wordlessly. The Wizard's sly eyes watched, moving between the two youngsters.

Yoder flinched at first, but found the bread put in his hand so he drew it closer and stared at Leeni with furrowed brows. She took up a broken piece of cheese next, holding it out to him and he tentatively took it as well. The boy bit into the bread, chewed quietly and swallowed it down with a drink from the water skin which he then offered to Leeni. She accepted it, trading for a piece of meat. Yoder couldn't take it anymore. "Why are you being nice NOW?" he asked bluntly. Leeni scowled at him, threw another chunk of bread at his chest and sat back to nibble on a piece of cheese.

The Wizard laughed outright, which made Leeni scowl more and Yoder look even more confused than he generally was. He picked up a small piece of meat with two fingers, tossing it into his mouth and chewing politely before he resumed smoking his pipe. Perrixstar thwapped Yoder in the back of the head with its tail, prompting the boy to remember to feed it.

While Yoder held up meat for Perrixstar to singe and ultimately devour, the other two ate quietly. Leeni staring sullenly at the red and white cloth under the basket of food and The Wizard happily looking between the two of them with that know-it-all smile on his sharp featured face.

Within a minute, he finally spoke. "The mudslide has cut off the road, we'll have to look for a way around it. That means northward rather than east."

Leeni looked up, her face full of concern. "The Kurn-Mines?! You've got to be kidding!"

The Wizard shook his head gravely. "I wish I were, but we're running out of time. Trying to cross the mudslide could delay us even more than circumnavigating it." He reasoned.

Yoder had no idea; he spoke up with a question. "Kurn-mines?"

Leeni frowned, not wanting to talk to the boy she was so angry with, but he deserved an answer. "Kurnites harvest minerals from the ground for their war machines and their furnaces or just to trade them with each other. The mines are disgusting, people get sick and die from exposure to some of the deeper ones. Plus, the worst Kurnites run the mines, they're cruel, evil people."

Yoder frowned now, listening to Leeni's explanation and letting it roll around in his head while he fed Perrixstar. "I'm with Leeni, it sounds dangerous," he said.

The Wizard shrugged. "Noted, but we're still going. We've no choice." And that was that. Yoder and Leeni exchanged a single glance, then she began to pointedly avoid him again.

Sixer seemed to wake up, but merely watched the humans consume their nutrients. He was particularly interested in how they shared them, not just between each other but with the small animal on Yoder's head as well. It found this to be acceptable, social behavior. Communal refueling for the good of the group.

When each had eaten their fill, Yoder sat back and rubbed his belly while Perrixstar settled in for a nap on his head. Leeni looked between Yoder and The Wizard, who both seemed content to leave the food there.

She narrowed her eyes. "I'm not cleaning up." She announced, offended. The Wizard raised a brow at that. Yoder looked at Leeni, perplexed. "It's not my job, I'm not your wife." She huffed, folding her arms over her chest. Yoder flushed red in the cheeks, looking toward The Wizard who stared back at him expectantly.

"What?" The boy asked. The Wizard's eyes shifted to the basket and blanket then back to him. Yoder groaned. "Fine…" He replied sullenly and rocked forward onto his knees to pack up the meats, cheese, bread, and apples into the basket again. He set it aside, folding up the cloth. Leeni seemed to relax.

Sixer interrupted the silence. "Why do you not work together to clean up?" It resonated the question, drawing attention from all three.

Leeni huffed. "Cause I'm an adventurer, not their serving girl." Her shoulders tensed up defensively. The Wizard shrugged, saying nothing at all.

Yoder smiled. "It's okay, I've got it."

But Sixer continued the inquiry. "You shared the food, should you not share the responsibility?" It asked again.

The Wizard finally glanced up at the giant over his shoulder. "I provided the food, which I shared with them." Yoder nodded to that, so did Leeni. Sixer fell silent, processing.

After a moment, it responded. "I understand. Thank you, Maker."

Once the meal was packed up, The Wizard stuffed it into his bottomless pocket item by item then worked up to his feet. Yoder and

Leeni rose, each preparing for the trip by checking their weapons. Yoder took a moment to stuff his drying gear into his pack before he slung it onto his shoulders. The three humans started north from the copse of trees, Yoder beckoning for Sixer to follow them. Sixer's spherical body cranked, extending the tubes of his legs until he was effectively standing then began to swing his weighted feet one by one after the group to keep pace. It took quite a while before the three of them were used to the loud thump or the creak of trees as the giant pushed between them.

Chapter Nine:
That's Disgusting!

Leaving Sixer behind in the tree line, Yoder, the Wizard, and Leeni all snuck up onto the ridgeline of grass on a hill that overlooked the venomous Kurn-mines. Once a thriving community on the very edge of Kurn and Halziyon, the mines have become a cesspool over time. Ores and minerals harvested from the earthen depths also dredged up acids and harmful chemicals that have poisoned both the land and its people, leaving the region a withered, gray husk of pollutants.

Railways crisscrossed the grounds, connecting the various excavated caverns to each other for passing carts between. Small hovels dot the landscape like pimples, tiny and whitish gray rounded tents that provide only the barest of security to those who dwell and toil here.

Fetid vagrants mill about the wastes between ponds and pools of fluids none are willing to touch themselves, fighting over what little precious metals and stones one can still gather in the wide, threatening maws left all over the land. The people murder each other without care, oft-times dumping their victims into the waste pools. Neither plant nor animal wish to tread upon this blighted place, much like the rest of the stripped land called Kurn.

Yoder pinched his nose, the stink and toxic vapors reaching his nose and making his eyes water. "Oh God, that's disgusting!" He groaned, Leeni fought to hold her lunch on the Wizard's other side. She retched awkwardly toward the grass, unable to speak for fear she might vomit in front of them.

The Wizard scowled instead, his face a dark mask of outrage. "Aye, an unfortunate and abused land lies before us." His eyes scanned the horizon, its miasmic cloud of acrid smoke like the top layer of a rotten cake. "We'll need to plan accordingly."

Leeni balked, slapping the Wizard's shoulder repeatedly for attention then pointed ahead at two grubby men in rags, hobbling a cart with a broken wheel along the central safe pathway. They were stopped by black armored guards with raised, gauntleted hands. The three watched an exchange that came to blows. Yoder's eyes widened in horror as the guards plunged a sword and spear each into the men, felling them without remorse. Worse still, the two guards dragged the cart to the side of the roadway and began to pick through its contents.

As The Wizard backed away from the hill, Leeni and Yoder followed suit until the horrible stench eased to fresh, clean air that all three sucked in hastily through deep breaths. They returned in due course to Sixer, whose blue light eyes opened wide as they approached.

"Analysis?" It resonated at the party.

Yoder flailed his fat arms. "HOW do we get through THAT? It's vile and full of lunatics! Not to mention guards who KILL you! We should go back, go around the other way or just cross the mud."

Leeni leaned on a tree, still green around her nonexistent gills while she clutched her middle in her arms. "He's right. It's impossible."

"Nothing is impossible, only uncomfortable." The Wizard replied, recovering far faster than his companions. "We'll need to cover ourselves, perhaps cut up the tent to make ragged cloaks."

Yoder protested. "But that's our tent! Where are we going to sleep… assuming there's fresh air somewhere in this shithole?!"

The Wizard waved him off dismissively. "I can fashion masks that will save us the ignominy of being noticed through our aversion to the smell, further hiding us as we pass." he said thoughtfully.

Leeni shook her head. "As if that'll get us past the guards in the first place."

While the two argued, Yoder was struck with an insight and looked at the large, round sphere that made up the core of Sixer's mass. He blinked twice, then pointed up at the construct. "What about Sixer? He's too big for a cloak and... you know, not a human."

Sixer's blue lights fixed on Yoder. "Thank you, Yoder. I appreciate your observation."

The Wizard shrugged. "He stays behind." The man simply stated, but Yoder swiveled with a glare.

"We're not leaving Sixer behind, he's one of us now and he's all alone besides." While the spheroid watched, the fat lad and his guide squared off for the first time. Even Leeni held her breath, wide eyed and watching.

The Wizard narrowed his eyes, turning on the boy. "If we must leave him to complete the mission, then that is what we will do." He said firmly, bringing his crystal-headed cane before him to set its tip in the soft ground like an uncompromising tutor.

Yoder's hands curled into fists at his sides. "I said No!" He yelled, his anger affecting his vocal control.

The Wizard snapped at him. "Mind your tone!" He instructed succinctly, but Yoder would have none of it.

"What if we need him?! Look at him, he's gigantic and strong but if we leave him here then who knows what'll happen to him. What if the guards notice?"

The Wizard began to speak but dropped off, his eyes sparked with the brilliance of a plan forming. "Ohh. Ohhhhh, my -boy-!"

The Wizard rushed forward, grasping one of Yoder's fists and shaking it so firmly that the boy's arm flopped about, and his jowly cheeks shook. "Genius, Yoder. Genius!"

Yoder blinked, stunned. "What? How? I mean, thanks but…. I don't get it." Sixer's plated head twitched left and right, observing the two males.

The Wizard smiled wide. "He's a distraction! HAH!" Yoder's eyes widened, so did Sixer's lights. Leeni scrunched her face up, but the Wizard went on. "Sixer begins his trek through the mines, drawing the guards' attention and creating chaos after we're on the road. We run ahead of him, acting as if we mean to outrun the havoc and once, we've cleared the minelands; we will deal with the guards who do not give up the chase!"

Yoder looked past The Wizard at Leeni, sharing in her distrust of this idea. "You're mad." He said, turning his eyes back on the man before him. "What if he gets hurt?"

Sixer resonated an interruption. "Yoder, I cannot be hurt as you understand it. I do not feel. My composition is primarily plating, servomechanisms, and my core processing unit. I may be damaged, but not harmed."

Yoder shook his head. "It doesn't matter, Sixer. If you're damaged and shut down, we can't move you. You're too big."

Sixer hummed gently. "I am grateful for your concern, friend. I am willing to do this for you, it is my analysis that your mission is very important if the maker deems it so."

The Wizard nodded soundly. "It's settled then." He smugly added, digging into his dimensional pocket with his left hand to root for the packed tent. "We shall act as the other Kurnish vermin until Sixer makes his approach then run with all our might ahead of him." He said, throwing the tent-roll onto the grass before crouching down to unfurl it. Leeni stared at Yoder with sympathy but lowered to help. Yoder turned on Sixer, looking up at his blue lights.

"Are you sure about this? What if you're the only one left of the Solarian Workers?"

Sixer was silent for a moment, his lights fixed on Yoder's face. "I appreciate you, Yoder." The construct stated in its deep, resonant tone. "If I am the last worker of Solaria, I will fulfill my duty to the makers."

Yoder frowned but heaved a sigh and reached up to pat the spheroid on its concave plating. "Okay."

A bell's toll of labor later, the tent was cut up into three cloaks. The third of which had a larger hood than the rest for Yoder would need to conceal Perrixstar on his head beneath it. Each of the three wrapped themselves in thick, sturdy cloth and covered their heads, though Perrixstar hissed at being constrained.

"We do not like this, Fat Slave."

Yoder huffed. "Deal with it, you'll like what's happening a lot less," he advised the creature as the three started toward the road.

Each pulled a strip of cloth over their mouths and noses, the fabric perfumed with rose oil and water that The Wizard kept for his own cleanliness. It worked, but the closer they all came to the bubbling swills; the more the terrible stink invaded around the cloth coverage. The Wizard walked ahead of Leeni and Yoder, hunched slightly and using his cane to add a pronounced limp to his movement. Yoder tried to act like he had a hunch, but only really seemed to stumble and wobble instead which Leeni tried not to laugh at.

The Kurnish guard stepped forward as they approached them, bringing their weapons to bear after conversing with each other. "HOLD." One called. "By order of the Black Vanguard, HOLD."

The Wizard stopped, huddling down some and peeking from the fold of the hood. "Why?" he asked in a false, high pitched and almost feminine tone. The first guard tensed, looked at the other guard and then turned his helmed head back to the disguised Wizard.

"Because." The guard stated, but his tone had a questioning lilt to it.

The Wizard grinned under his cowl, maintaining the voice. "Because Why?" he asked again. Both guards exchanged glances, the spearman shrugged black plated shoulders. The speaking guard went silent then suddenly perked up.

"Oh! I remember! Because Garrick Thain, God-King of Kurn said so!" He stated proudly. "Now, what do you want?" The spearman straightened up, keeping the deadly point aimed at the huddled form before them.

"Make some money. Yesss. Find gold, silver, coal! Ehehehehe." Leeni covered her mouth to restrain the giggle bubbling up at The Wizard's witch-like laugh. Yoder snorted but stifled himself.

The lead guard lowered his sword slightly. "Good luck with that, you old crone. Should let me skewer you here rather than die in the mines of exposure."

The Wizard cooed from his cowl. "Sweet boy, I'll take me chances." And he began to limp forward when the Spearman cried out.

"What is THAT?!" The other guard's sword shook in his hand, lifting higher as a horrible clanking, metallic groaning erupted behind the three facing the guards.

Sixer swung his leg tubes, launching foot plates forward quickly from the tree line. He extended his arm tubes out and upward, wiggling them like serpents and making his wide metal mitts thrash about above him. The vagrants of Kurn screamed and shouted at the monstrous sight, scattering like rats. The Wizard began to run, but the sword guard grabbed him around the middle and pulled him back from the road. Leeni and Yoder panicked, running past as the Wizard struggled in the guard's hold. The Spearman launched his weapon into the air at the monster bearing down on them, watching it clink off the metal plating and fall harmlessly to the road. He screamed, diving to the ground and curled up into a ball.

Yoder and Leeni flew ahead as fast as they could, followed by the caterwauling Sixer. None knew where they were going. For a moment, The Wizard stopped struggling in the one guard's arms and simply stared in bewilderment. When his wits returned, he raised his cane and bounced the crystal head off the guard's helmet.

"Get off me, boy!" he screeched as old womanly as he could. The guard let go and the Wizard dashed forward fleetly, chasing the construct chasing the teens. "Eeeeeeek!" He keened, remaining in character.

The sword guard straightened his helm, watching the disguised Wizard run off then crossed the roadway to his companion's huddle form. A kick to the rump brought the former spearman up to a sitting position.

"That was weird." One said to the other.

The spear guard nodded. "You're crazy, you could've been killed and for what? Some ugly old hag."

The sword guard shrugged, looking back at the chaos of the giant spherical machine rushing around wildly. "She reminded me of my mum," he said wistfully.

Yoder stumbled over his cloak, running out of breath the more he got lost in the wild hustle of the moment. Everything looked the same, smelled the same putrid way, he couldn't figure which way was the right way.

"Go!" He called to Leeni, diving to the side to roll across the grimy dirt and lay there catching his breath.

Sixer's massive footplate slammed into the ground nearby and its great bulk soared closer. Yoder heaved air, staring up at the sky when one of Sixer's large hands swooped down on him. He screamed, girlishly frightened as the hand scooped him off the ground and the world went topsy turvy. Perrixstar yowled above him, tumbling around his neck then getting caught in the pouch of his tent-cloak's back. The creature scrambled, clawing wildly to get its bearings. Yoder cried through the pain, his stomach lurching as he was swung about above Sixer's plated head.

Leeni ran hard ahead of Sixer, eyes wide as she glanced back and saw the giant machine swinging Yoder around in its hand. "OH GOD" She cried out, running even harder out of proper fear when the cloaked form of The Wizard came rushing to her side with inhuman speed.

"Left!" He called, driving Leeni and the construct behind her to the appropriate direction. Carts were overturned, Kurnish folk scrambled over each other and into their tents while random guards watched but curiously did not try to stop the monster ravaging the roadways.

As the two found the road out of the mine fields finally, they were obstructed by a stone wall and closed gate. Three black armored guards stood before the closed gate with weapons drawn, another spear, an axe, and sword. Upon the gates parapets were two guards with bows aimed at the giant creature trying to destroy the countryside.

Leeni and the Wizard skid to a stop and ditched aside, both rolling across the slimy ground as Sixer careened forward at the gateway. Arrows were loosed, clinking off Sixer's plates and Yoder bellowed in pain and terror overhead which did little for the guardsmen's morale. Still, they held their ground and Sixer came to an awkward and confused stop. He'd expected them to run, of course. The construct lowered its limbs slowly as it cranked in its leg tubes to sit on its footplates. Yoder was laid on the ground where he puked most embarrassingly all over it. Perrixstar wriggled and crawled up his jerking body til it could shove the hood enough to get its tiny lizard head out into open air. It hissed angrily.

Leeni rushed toward Yoder, checking him and the faerie dragon worriedly while the Wizard threw back his hood and rose to stand. "I wasn't expecting a wall! Who builds a bloody wall...oh right. It's Kurn." The Wizard scoffed. "Gentlemen! Stand aside and raise the gate or my machine here will destroy you all!" he called out politely, but with a threat in his tone. Sixer loomed as ominously as he could, which was quite good given his great size and alien shape.

The Axe Guard took a threatening step forward, gripping the long haft with both hands. "Call off your monster or we will kill you all! How's that sound? Huh?!" He bellowed back almost childishly.

The Wizard rolled his eyes. "Kurns." He sighed. "Look, idiot. My machine trumps your axe. Your arrows didn't even leave a mark. Go ahead, look harder. Stand aside."

The axe guard leaned forward, appearing to inspect the massive construct before rocking back and looking behind himself to his companions. Yoder finally stopped puking, letting Leeni watch the exchange with confused concern.

After a brief conference, the bowmen trained their newly nocked arrows on The Wizard instead. The Axeman called out "We'll shoot you then." as one might expect from such haphazard stand-offs to play out.

The Wizard took the threat very seriously, darting towards Sixer's footplate. "Go!" He called to the worker drone, who flung his other footplate toward the Axeman. The man leaped away in fright as the plate thunked into the dirt, Sixer cranking its spheroid body toward the guards and gate again.

Arrows were loosed, glancing off the machine's plates once more. Yoder's wits recovered enough to understand the fight and he crawled to his feet while drawing his sword.

"We have to help!" he called out to Leeni as he rushed forward to aid Sixer. Leeni flicked her short blades out instantly, moving in behind Yoder's charge while Perrixstar hissed at all the commotion but couldn't get itself out of the hood, so the dragon merely clung to Yoder's hair.

The Wizard was spared an arrow to the knee as he ducked behind Sixer's forward momentum, whirling around to bring his cane up in front of him. He began to chant in a language long lost, a language only the machine could interpret but it had other things to do. Wind roiled around him, fluttering the heavy cloak with winds gathering around his booted feet.

The crystal embedded in his cane began to glow faintly, a greenish light that steadily and slowly grew brighter and brighter the more The Wizard chanted. They had no more time to waste, he knew. All the mistakes made had cost them time. But he couldn't worry about that. His concentration focused on the words, the gathering energy forming at the crystal on his cane. He used the words of reality like a poet uses them to weave beautiful narrative.

His eyes closed, focusing his mind on the singular path. The magic that swelled around him like a tornado now, funneling and fueling the brightly beaming crystal until he was ready to release its full force at a single target. One that the Wizard visualized in his mind's eye. Spellcasting of this magnitude was dangerous, even for him. It required great care and control.

This was Solarian wizardry at its purest, from a time when the first kingdom grasped the infinite and wrestled it into the palms of their hands. A world that Sixer came from, along with many other wondrous splendors. A kingdom now long gone from the planet, leaving all this madness in its absence. The Wizard felt the spell complete, reality warping before him.

Chapter Ten:
You could've warned us!

Yoder's first real battle was one he had little chance to think about, his only desire was to aid his new friend. Fat feet thumped on the dusty, dead ground as the corpulent boy charged around Sixer's left flank with the small and speedy Leeni on his heels. The axeman raised his weapon at the large mechanical creature, but saw the boy come rushing around the side and shifted his greaved footing.

Sixer's arms extended as long as they could from the spheroid shell that was its core with loud cranking sounds. Wide, metal hands reached for the bowmen on the parapets to protect his companions from their dangerous arrows. Each arrowman moved to dodge the swiping palms that grasped for them, one ducking below while the other panicked and dove off the side of the parapet behind the wall with a scream.

The spearman thrust forward at Yoder, trying to halt his charge but Leeni intercepted the wicked point with an effortless spin around Yoder's back and an arcing swing of her short blade. Utilizing the training she had learned in her time with her last troupe of adventurers, the skillful girl's sword connected and drove the spear away and upward. She followed through, twisting around to slash across the spearman and force him to jump back from engaging.

Yoder let out a scream, less girlish and more intense to steel what courage he had in the adrenaline that guided him to charge a knight in full armor with a large axe. That thought stung him and the boy hesitated, his booted feet skidding in the dead earth underneath. The axeman saw his opening and thrust forward, bringing the axe downward but Yoder clenched his eyes shut and threw up his arm in fear of the gruesome weapon only to be saved by the wolf's head shield strapped to it. The Axe clacked loudly off the polished shield, but without a hand's grip; the shield swung downward with the force of the blow.

Yoder couldn't think, couldn't bring himself to raise his sword like he should. His arms felt heavy and numb, his blue eyes snapping open at the sound of axe against shield to see the looming, black armored knight no more than a foot away from him. Perrixstar clutched his hair in its little claws, pulling itself up onto Yoder's head again and instinctually stretched its neck forward to release its gout of flame into the axeman's visor. The knight cried out in fright, dropping his axe and stumbling backward from the heat of dragon's fire and somehow, Yoder seemed to become purely clear.

These weren't unbeatable enemies, they were men. Men like him. He huffed for air, finding his lungs filling easily then glanced down at the sword in his hand. His father's sword, the wolf pack charging up the blade, shone in the sunlight overhead. He could do this, he had to do this to protect his friends, to fulfil his destiny, to save the whole of the world.

Leeni fought off the spearman, twirling and driving him back toward the wall with her fast swordswork. She had always practiced with the spare longsword she'd be given, the heavy blade that she could barely hold up or the ranger's bow when her companions let her use it. But these weapons were hers, lighter, easier to wield and just as deadly. She knew how to use them through practice with Yoder the other day, yet the lack of weight made her stumble here and there. Only her speed saved her, keeping the lancer awkwardly trying to recover his pole as she slashed and smacked it about and drew closer and closer to her target. The question she had yet to answer was what she should do when she got there?

Was she a killer? Her mind became distracted by the question, the implication. She had slain beasts for food for the party, but never struck down a person before. Not that she would ever admit any of this to the others, but Leeni Vex was afraid to end this fight. The spearman took advantage of the distraction, switching the weapon with a drawback and swing out with the back end that slapped the girl in her middle. She was shocked, her air rushed out of her lungs in a pained groan as they turned terrifyingly cold in her chest. She couldn't breathe, her blades fell from her hands and the world began to spin like a cyclone.

Sixer successfully stopped one of the archers, but the other had evaded his grasp. Blue lights in his face-sphere aimed at the ducked archer and both his wibbly-wobbly arms swung about then came crashing down on the parapet with strong intent. The risk of threat to his compatriots was still dangerous with this human upon the high ground, so the machine showed him no mercy. The archer screamed at the descending metal hands, crouching down and raising his arms over himself only to be summarily squished by the crashing, heavy weights.

In dealing with the archers, the mechanical Sixer had left himself open to the sword guard who was circling around to find the foppish Wizard. His sword raised, tip aimed ahead of him, the soldier crept one foot at a time in a wide arc to see his quarry before he decided how to strike. When he found The Wizard chanting over the crystal that was embedded in the head of his cane, the swordsman dropped his sword and ran. The last any of the group saw of him was the armored man clanking away from the fight bellowing "WIZARD!" as loudly as he could.

Yoder, in front of Sixer's spheroid mass, started to raise his sword with uncertainty over the axeman when he heard the girlish groan behind him. He looked back, did a double take and then turned his back on the fallen knight.

"LEENI!" He cried, charging toward her with his sword high and his shield arm raised this time. He caught the hand strap to secure it as well, his mind clear on his actions: save his friend. The spearman twirled the pole, catching it with the vicious point aimed down at the girl who gasped on her hands and knees before him.

The large lad ducked his head, finding strength in his fear and need to save the girl who seemed to hate him. His boots pounded lifeless dust as he surged forward, and the spear came down just as Yoder reached Leeni's side. The tip caught on the steel rim of the shield, just barely in time and with Yoder's forward momentum; it bowed hard then snapped free of the spearman's hand. As the pole flipped end over end above him, Yoder slammed his weight, sword, and shield into the spearman with fury. A second slower and Leeni would've been dead! The soldier bounced back against the wall then released a gurgling wail as Yoder drove into him. When the boy looked up, the spearman's mouth spilled blood down his chin and Yoder saw the tip of his father's sword stuck fast in the kurnishman's throat.

Red ran down the blade, spilling off the edges as it reached the hilt and Yoder watched the impaled man die making strangled, mewling noises. His hand began to tremble, releasing the sword and he backed up a step with his mouth hanging open in shellshock. The soldier slid down the wall, sword leaning downward as the weight pulled in his craw.

"I...I…. I'm sorry!" he moaned, throwing himself down on his knees by the dying man and reaching out with shivering hands toward the red blood flowing freely out of his neck. "Oh my god. I'm sorry! I didn't…" But did he? All that courage, that sense of purpose to save Leeni meant what? He had a sword; he knew what they were for. Guilt overpowered the boy as he watched the light fade in the soldier's eyes.

With Yoder and Leeni both stunned, it fell to Perrixstar to save the day for while Leeni tried to gain her air and Yoder struggled with the murder he'd committed; the axeman cometh. The knight had been forgotten, but he grasped his axe and charged after the fat bastard that had killed his friend and he was drawing back the axe to make his blow when the faerie dragon turned around and rose up on Yoder's head. Its neck extended fully upward, body rearing back on its hind legs and its little front claws curled up against its breast scales. Those shimmering wings fanned out wide, making the tiny beast as big as it could be. The axeman feared another gout of flame, turning his helmed head away and in that moment, the little dragon struck.

Perrixstar whipped around, lashing out with its tail and that wicked barb on the end of it sank into the knight's exposed neck. It bit deep into the throbbing artery, pulled free without remorse by the dragon's bodily twist back. The Axeman grabbed at his neck, dropping to his knees and once again; that axe fell with him. Unlike the spearman's wound, the knight's neck pumped an arc of blood then the rest seemed to pour from the open wound down into his armor and quickly pool at his knees.

Yoder and Leeni both heard the clunk of armor, looking over to see the knight's life run like a faucet from his neck. Each looked horrified at the terrible display and even though Leeni couldn't breathe, she felt like she might puke all the same. Yoder probably would have as well, but The Wizard's spell suddenly finished. A gust of hurricane winds flashed out around Sixer's mass like the roar of a massive dragon, his arms were caught in the gale force and wobbled wildly toward the wall and its gate. Yoder grabbed for Perrixstar on his head, pulling the dragon down into his chest behind his shield as the wind rose and Leeni curled up on the gray ground. The dying knight was blown away, his body crashed into the gate which groaned in protest. A moment later, the lock snapped, and the gate bent with a louder resound before it tore free of the stone and flopped a good twenty steps away.

The structural integrity of the gateway, parapets, and wall were compromised by the gate breaking loose, the stone starting to crumble then topple over completely in a cacophony of destructive force then the winds died away as quickly as they came. The group of odd adventurers began to pick themselves up off the ground.

"What in God's name was -that-?!" Yoder bellowed. The Wizard bounced out from behind Sixer, whose arms were like limp noodles extended as far as they'd go and lying serpentine amidst the rubble.

"Me! That was me, saving our lives, opening the gate and whatnot." The foppish man beamed proudly.

"Are you insane?!" Yoder yowled at the man while Perrixstar climbed free of his embrace and pulled itself up over the rim of Yoder's shield.

The Wizard frowned at this reaction. "...possibly? The spell took some time, but I see everyone's fine, bit more than I expected actually,"

He added, admiring his handiwork in the absolute devastation of what had once been a wall and portcullis.

"You could've warned us!" Yoder replied, admonishing The Wizard with high-strung anger. "And we're not fine! Leeni's hurt, I killed someone accidentally and my dragon is psychotic!"

Perrixstar flapped its wings, rising into the air with a hiss. "Whose dragon? You're MY fat slave." It said, turning a circle to bob in the air and look down at the blonde boy. "That stupid human would've cut you down, so I killed it. That…." Its lizard head thrust toward what was left of the soldier Yoder had stabbed, half covered in stone chunks with the wolf's run sword protruding and wobbling out of it still. "…stupid human would have killed the female slave and you killed it first. That is what we do. You turned more stupid, fat slave. Don't do that again."

Yoder closed his mouth, neck craning back as if the words the dragon spoke had slapped him in the face. It was right, he had saved Leeni by killing that man just like it had saved him by killing the knight. They protected each other. Yoder looked down, trying to process through the horrible experience and the faerie dragon's warped rationale when The Wizard cleared his throat.

"Helloooooooo. MAGIC. Big spell, blew the gate away." He thrust his hands and cane toward the wreckage. "We can proceed through Kurn now, quickly. Very quickly, yes? More guards coming, I would say. WHY IS NOBODY IMPRESSED?!" He finished, stomping his soft boots in the gray, lifeless dirt amidst the dust cloud.

Sixer's head-sphere swiveled a full one hundred and eighty degrees, blue lights widening for maximum scanning of the horizon through the cloud surrounding them. "The Maker is correct; we must proceed before we are detained." He resonated from his core chamber, cranking his arms back from the ground.

Yoder sighed, working his way up to his feet then moved to help Leeni up too. "You alright?" he asked gently, holding her arm with his shield hand and grasping around her middle with the other.

The girl pushed him away, staggering up to her feet with dirty air in her lungs that made her cough. "I'm fine! Leave me alone!" She hoarsely snapped, taking an unsure step forward and finding her feet worked just fine so she proceeded angrily ahead to gather her weapons.

Yoder glared at the back of her head. "Of all the ungrateful.... then.... What is wrong with you?!" The young man asked angrily, causing the chestnut-haired girl to turn on him fiercely.

"I don't need you to save me! I can handle myself!" Leeni said, fighting back the tears that made her want to run away from him and all of this. "I'm an adventurer, better than you are. I know what I'm doing, okay? OKAY?!" Yoder glowered. As ever, his dream of being a hero was sullied by her when he was only trying to help. It was disappointing for the boy, never realizing that she wasn't angry with him at all.

"Okay! Fine!" He turned, kicked a small hunk of stone and stalked off to pull his sword from the corpse while grousing in a way that only Yoder could do well. His anger made it easier to ignore the body, shoving his blade into its scabbard at his hip and turning away quickly. "Well? Are we going or not?" Yoder tersely called out, stepping up on a piece of debris to cross over when he paused and noticed the axe handle sticking up from a pile nearby.

While he dug it out, The Wizard muttered to himself about powerful Solarian magic and how hard it was to learn such a spell much less channel the energy to cast it effectively as he rounded Sixer's base and hopped from rock to rock over the rubble that was once a gateway. Leeni did the same, silently angry for a great many reasons she kept in her head. Finally, the boy yanked the axe free and propped the short pole haft of it on his shoulder.

"I could wield an axe, shouldn't be that hard" he thought to himself as he joined the others climbing the wreck.

Upon the other side, The Wizard and Leeni were both marching onward, but Yoder looked back into the dust cloud. He took six large steps to the side then yelled out "Clear! Throw your foot or step or whatever you do!"

A moment later, one of Sixer's weight-like feet soared out of the cloud and crashed into the dirt in front of the boy who waited while the machine cranked across the devastation; scraping the undercarriage of its spheroid base against jutting rock.

"Come on, let's go." Yoder said to his new friend, turning to follow his other companions way ahead. "I've never left Halziyon before," he commented idly to Sixer, who paced itself to the boy in order to keep him company.

Sixer hummed, cranking its mass from one weight to another alongside the lad. "I am unfamiliar with this territory; the geographical location should be plainsland but this kingdom of Kurn is not registered in my data archive." Yoder shrugged, axe blade bobbing as he walked. Perrixstar swooped down and landed on his head, but he paid no mind. The creature had saved him. For all its insults; it had been there when he needed it.

"I don't know much about it either." The boy said, drawing in breath to call out ahead. "Hey! Where did Kurn come from?!"

The Wizard stopped stalking ahead, spinning about on his dirty, but still fine boots. "Will you -shut- -up-?" Accentuating the two words. "We are invading a country run by an absolute prat who happens to be just as skilled in magicks as I am, we might be pursued by an entire squadron of knights at this very moment and you want to bellow trivia at me!" he said, scolding the lad.

Yoder frowned, breathed out audibly through his nose then looked up at Sixer. "Maybe we'll ask when we make camp…"

The Wizard turned about, stomping quickly across the barren sands after Leeni who had traveled on ahead. Sixer's eye lights widened and shrank as he watched the Maker curiously, then rotated his head sphere and tipped those lights down to look upon his companion.

"It is best." The machine resonated in its tinny tone. "I will scan our surroundings for signs of pursuit." Yoder nodded, falling into wary silence and his own inner thoughts. A man was dead because of him, but the cause he felt was righteous even if Leeni was mad at him for it. The trek through the wastes of Kurn would be ample time to think through it all.

Chapter Eleven:
Blithering Imbeciles

Atolicus Grehner looked over the rubble that was the east gate of Kurn with a scowl. As commander of the northern reach, in charge of the Kurn-mines, this would fall squarely on his pauldron clad shoulders. Surrounded by black armored Kurnishmen making up his escort phalanx, Atolicus sat astride his black mare, Augustine, and rubbed at the bristly beard upon his chin. His head was adorned with a finned black metal helm to match his plated armor, but the red cape that billowed down his broad back was what separated him from the soldiers, other than the horse he rode naturally.

Gauntleted hands lifted the helmet off his head, revealing behind the chain veil attached over the back of his neck that Atolicus Grehner was very much bald. A thin ring of hair was left, which he shaved down to the scalp rather than wear out of pride for his grizzly, vicious appearance. A wide nose rested over his angry, pursed lips and above the nose were two beady, dark brown eyes to match the coloration of his chin-hair. He made a clucking sound with his tongue, lips parted to suck air between his teeth before he hefted his helm up high and threw it down at the nearest soldier in his entourage. The helmet clanged off the soldier's own, knocking the man over. The other soldiers around the fallen man glanced at each other, but kept their mouths shut.

"Who the hell did this?!" Grehner barked crudely. "And how?!" He added with a snarl, throwing one leg over his saddle to drop down to the ground with a clattering of metal. He stood, lip curling as he looked around at all of his men. "Well? GO FIND OUT!" He roared, hauling off and kicking the soldier he'd knocked down squarely in the middle as hard as he could. The victim of his wrath bounced, falling flat and coughing in the gray, lifeless dirt while the rest of the soldiery ran from their leader to fulfill his wish and get away from his violence.

Left alone, Atolicus stomped closer to the rubble and examined the mess thoroughly. His beady eyes glowered harder as he noticed the bodies of his men amidst the fallen, broken stones, not to mention the big red spot where the squad leader had emptied his heart's blood upon the earth. He was about to kick the corpse when the hairs on his face and neck raised in that alarming way they tend to do when something terrifying is about to happen. He spun around, reaching for the leather wrapped handle of his longsword, but stopped himself from pulling it free of its lacquered scabbard.

"My King." Atolicus said suddenly, bending a knee and prostrating himself.

From within a haze, like high heat on desert sand, came Garrick Thain, stepping onto the Kurn-mines dead earth with one well-oiled and shiny black boot then the other. Each boot folded down at the cuff, revealing crimson velvet on the inside. The king of Kurn wore fine, black robes inlaid with crimson thread and gold clasps over a white silk shirt and soft tanned brown trousers. His face was marked by age but regal all the same with a thin, short nose and both strong cheekbones and jawline. His hair was brown, short and styled to a curled point upon his prominent forehead.

"Atolicus. What is the meaning of this?" he said in a rich timbre.

Atolicus kept his head bowed, resting his forward arm upon his knee. "Begging your pardon, Sovereign Thain. I don't know yet. My men are questioning the miners as we speak. Whatever it was, it destroyed the entire gate and gained entry into Kurn proper."

Garrick Thain rolled his doe brown eyes, eyes that would no doubt be thought of as soft and gentle if they were not fitted into the skull of the most reviled mage of the lower midlands.

"I can see that, Captain. Rise." He commanded, lazily waving a hand full of gold rings; each set with a different hued stone. Atolicus stood up immediately but waited for further instruction.

"Magic is the cause." Garrick Thain continued, walking past the Knight-Captain toward the wreckage of his kingdom's guard post. "Powerful magic, I can still feel its essence all around us. I could feel it the moment it was cast."

Atolicus turned around, following his Majesty's movements. "So that's why you've come." The captain said, which caused Garrick Thain to fix him with a withering side-eye.

"Do I need a reason to move about my own lands now, Captain Grehner?" He asked rhetorically with threat.

Atolicus stepped back defensively, shaking his bearded head. "No, my king! Of course not!"

Garrick Thain ignored him, sweeping his gaze across the devastation thoughtfully. Solarian magic. That meant the Mirrored Circle had infiltrated his kingdom, but he knew not to what end. The king of Kurn turned, intent on addressing his captain when Atolicus' men returned in haste. They all stopped suddenly at the sight of Garrick Thain standing tall and proud before the wreckage, then dropped to their knees.

"Your Majesty!" The men said in unison, bowing their heads. Garrick Thain looked to Atolicus with expectation.

"Report!" Atolicus barked at his squadron after staring at his king and waiting for a command, only to realize a tad too slow that he'd been silently given one. The soldiers kept their heads down, knelt in the gray dirt but the first among them spoke up.

"Sir! The miners report that a monster chased them through the railways. Most are too afraid to leave their hovels."

Atolicus growled while Garrick Thain watched on quietly. "And? No one saw who destroyed our gate?!" The captain snarled.

The lead soldier shook his helmed head. "No, Sir!"

"Blithering Imbeciles! I hate this god damned territory. Every single one of those miscreants is useless!" Atolicus bellowed, grasping his sword and tearing it furiously from its scabbard as he stalked toward the reporting soldier. "If I had my way, I'd burn the lot of them to the ground and..." He was cut off by a very audible but unassuming cough, his black eyes going wide, and his stomping gait stopped short. Atolicus turned toward Garrick Thain, lowering his sword tip toward the dusty ground. "For-forgive me, Your Majesty. I...err..."

Garrick Thain shook his head. "Unnecessary, Captain. The mines have been useless to me for many cycles now." He said, unconcerned. The king strode toward Atolicus and his squadron. "You would be well within your rights to burn the mines to ash.... or...." Garrick Thain's eyebrows rose in a suggestive manner. "You could put your attention to finding me the mage who cast the spell that destroyed our border. Assign your guardsmen to use the miners to rebuild the wall and gate while you are on this most hallowed mission for your king."

Atolicus Grehner lifted his free hand, stroking gloved fingers over his bristly beard. His bushy eyebrows raised, lowered, raised again as he mulled it all over then awkwardly asked in a softer tone. "Is that...what you want me to do, Your Majesty?"

Garrick Thain resisted the urge to immolate the captain in front of his men, closing his eyes and drawing in a heavy breath to calm his nerves. Atolicus was an idiot, like so many of his military leaders and subordinates were. If Garrick Thain didn't know better, he would blame the incompetence on his own overwhelming might and intellect. "Yes, Captain. That is what I want you to do."

"Right then! You heard the king!" Atolicus bellowed at his platoon. "Fetch the horses and load the wagon! You three, rally the miners out of their holes and get them moving the stones aside. Now! We'll track down this monster and his mage and make them dead!" The soldiers rose quickly, giving a cheer, then turned away to make for the guard barracks in one of the old mines. When they were gone, he turned back to Garrick Thain. "Beg your pardon, Majesty. We'll be in pursuit within three bell's tolls, once the rubble's been cleared."

Garrick Thain nodded firmly. His left hand raised, arcing this way and that way in swooping gestures to paint a symbol through the air. The rings on his fingers gathered energy into them, guided by his hand's motions until another distortion haze appeared in front of him.

"See that you are, Captain Grehner. I want that mage's head. Immediately."

Atolicus nodded firmly, bowing his head and thumping his chest with a gauntlet-clad fist. "As you command."

Garrick Thain smiled faintly, turned to the distorting haze fully then glanced back. "Oh, and Captain?" He said, drawing Atolicus Grehner's gaze up from the ground. "To be clear. Order your men to kill the miners when the wall is completed. Leave their bodies in the fetid pools."

Through the distortion, the King strode and with a single step traversed nearly one hundred miles to Garrilond, the sprawling city surrounding Thain Keep; the seat of his power in Kurn. Garrilond, so named for the ruler himself, was a testament to supreme dictatorship. A bleak cityscape of tall, dirty buildings in good repair but decidedly not beautiful. Drab like the soil on which it stands, the land was stripped when Thain rose to power, and those minerals were used to construct the square housing communities and Thain Keep itself. Here, no one man was better than another save for Garrick Thain.

The citizens were given bread and water drums weekly, overseen by the authority of the Black Vanguard; Thain's personal army. Soldiers were given permission to take what they wished from the people in exchange for protection and basic amenities. It was a simple life for the Kurnish people, who toiled in menial labors and trades for the benefit of the country alone. Families lived in small apartments within the large structures, dictated by the Black Vanguard's housing edicts as handed down by Garrick Thain himself.

An unfortunate side effect of his style of rule was that the Kurnish people had become, over time, very, very dumb. With their only requirement for living being subservience and labor, the two generations that had grown under Garrick Thain's iron fist did so without creativity, inspiration, and spirit. Garrilond alone provided for ten thousand souls who marched blindly through their lives either working bellows and anvils, baking bread, harvesting water or defending the country and that, as they say, was it. There were no Kurnish poets, no Kurnish music, and no Kurnish culture. Radical thinking of any kind was beaten out of the individual, all for the glory of Kurn's civility.

This had been how Garrick Thain rose to power. Upon the backs of the destitute, he had cultivated an army of wayward wretches with the promise of food, shelter, and comfort then turned that army into a military hive mind with him alone at its epicenter. Halziyon and the Mirrored Circle chose to leave the dangerous king of Kurn alone, for he inadvertently brought peace to the region by taking the indigent with him. Once the council of Halziyon realized the danger of his political offers and their effects upon people, the damage was already done.

Thain Keep loomed in the center of the city, the highest point of the horizon. A twelve-floor testament to his rule, it was circular, made of sturdy stone reinforced with manufactured steel and every window on the first eight floors could be opened and used as a vantage point by Black Vanguard snipers to defend it. Even the Mirrored Circle had to admit, it was the most impregnable building ever designed by man in a post-Solarian era. Each window was decorated with Thain's battle standard hanging from its ledge, a black shield and crossed swords on a field of crimson and outlined in gold. Not the color, but actual gold.

Within the eight main floors of the tower, the Black Vanguard kept their barracks and monitored the activity of the keeps staff as they cleaned, prepared lavish meals from Thain's personal gardens and livery, and served at the King's leisure. Only soldiers lived within those walls on the second-floor barracks and every servant was required to pass through those barracks and be checked before they may ascend. Each floor denoted higher rank and privilege, starting with military officer barracks and ending with High Arbiter Loew Marchand who advised the King personally. In truth, the word 'advise' was something of a misnomer: Marchand took orders directly from the King but advising sounded more official.

Above the High Arbiter's floor was the royal dining hall and the royal library, leading onward up to the four floors reserved only for Garrick Thain himself. The laboratory where Thain practiced his magic, designing many of the Black Vanguard's war machines and weapons. Thain's personal chambers were next, followed by a floor above that no servant nor guard dared to tread and then the observatory floor where Garrick Thain could scry upon his entire kingdom with a series of looking glasses and magical mirrors.

This was where his portal took him, folded boots landing on the smooth stone floor. He walked into the center of the room, lit only by ambient light from windows cut into the top floor every few feet for optimal visual range. Hanging above the center was a large crystal formation, the biggest that the Kurn-mines could excavate in their day. It was suspended by heavy, thick chains and a clinch of steel around the lower spike to keep it suspended in the air.

With a wave of his ring-laden hand in a specific pattern, the energy of the crystal was drawn into the gemstones on each finger and Garrick Thain used that power to fuel a fresh scrying spell. The casting ended with him placing his hand over his face and parting the index and pinky finger from the others to reveal his doe eyes, which flared brightly. The King of Kurn then walked to the first of many windows and looked out for miles and miles from its opening.

He stared across his dead landscape to the Kurn-mines, watching his soldiers whip the miners to spur them to clear the debris faster. He looked to the south of the mine, scanning the forest's edge until he noticed three horses grazing, tied to a tree but unguarded and further still to what appeared to be a mudslide. No doubt from the heavy storm the day previous. Garrick Thain's lips pursed, stepping away to another window to continue his search all the way to the steelworks where his forges burned hot, and smoke billowed into the sky like a dark god.

Nothing. The King turned and hurried to another window, growing agitated. His magic eyes scanned from the rubble of the gate once more but now across the dunes, catching sight of thick imprints in the dead earth. Large, rounded imprints that could be the tracks of the monster which terrorized the Kurn-mines and destroyed his wall. Garrick Thain's frustration flared when the trail simply stopped at the apex of one dune. His gaze swept onward but found no further tracks.

"Impossible...," he muttered to himself, sliding his vision back to where the tracks had stopped only to find three more down from the top of the dune.

His eyes narrowed, focusing more acutely. Three new imprints in the dirt, but no sign of the beast. His mind raced, trying to search for an answer to the mystery when a new imprint appeared ahead of the rest. Garrick Thain smirked suddenly, realizing just what was transpiring.

"Clever mage," he remarked to himself. A spell to hide his course, almost foolproof if it weren't for the crusty, gray dirt the intruder and his monster traveled across.

The King of Kurn quickly descended from the observatory to his lab, crossing the candlelit floor to a table adorned in crimson cloth and open tomes. He motioned to the black candle on the table.

"Igni" Garrick Thain commanded, the ruby on his middle finger flaring as the candle tip sputtered a small flame. Smoke billowed from the flame, forming a thick cloud. "Captain Grehner." He said to the cloud which roiled and swirled into the hazy shape of a bearded head wearing a rounded helm.

"My King?" The shadowy shape replied.

Garrick Thain scowled. "To the west, follow the dunes straight until you find deep, large footprints in the dirt. These tracks will lead you to your quarry. Be warned, they are cloaked in a spell of hiding."

Atolicus Grehner's shade nodded firmly. "Yes, Your Majesty. The rubble will be cleared in the next bell's toll, we will proceed as ordered." He said to which Garrick Thain nodded.

"Good." He waved his hand, extinguishing the candle and banishing the dark cloud that bore Grehner's face. He turned away from it, looking over the shelves of amazing artifacts and oddities he kept in his laboratory while ruminating on the cloaking spell being used to hide from his scrying. A sly mage and accomplished too.

Striding back up to the observatory, Garrick Thain returned to the window and recast the spell of farsight once more. He found the end of the trail of tracks, then inscribed in the air before him another symbol. The emerald on his pinky began to glow, followed by the amethyst on his thumb. His perspective altered, changing from the visual human spectrum to one that could see magic. His land was a black void of nothing, but he could see the infiltrators clear as day.

A small round mote of power moved in an odd way. It remained still, then shot forward by many feet only to stop still again then burst forward once more. Beside the oddly moving orb was a small, thin line that swung back and forth on its course. A magical weapon of some sort, the King deduced. But at the head of the two was a veritable sun of power, bright and radiating magical energy like a star in the night sky. An energy Garrick Thain recognized instantly, his face overshadowing with anger.

"You…," he whispered with deadly intent.

Chapter Twelve:
That's Impossible

Under the magical scrutiny of Garrick Thain, The Wizard and Leeni crossed dune after dune unending in a forced march followed by Yoder, Perrixstar curled upon his head, and Sixer's slow gait. The Wizard felt a shiver run down his spine, looking to the south with narrowed eyes until Leeni called attention to it.

"What is it?" she asked, drawing The Wizard's gaze away. He turned his head, shrugged his shoulders and offered a smile up.

"Nothing as far as I can see. Welcome to Kurn. A whole lot of nothing."

Yoder heard this, wiping sweat from his forehead with the sleeve of his shirt which was already soaked from the long walk. "How much farther?!" He whined, regretting the decision to bring the very awesome axe along on this trek. It's added weight made his arm and shoulder hurt.

The Wizard grit his teeth, his ward's whine always grating on his nerves. "Barring any troubles, half a day if we keep moving."

Yoder groaned. "Alright…" He said somberly, forcing himself to keep moving.

"The alternative is to stop and let the Kurnish forces catch up to us, if you prefer." The Wizard snapped, drawing a disapproving look from Leeni. He sighed, shook his head and added. "I'm tired too, but we will reach the Razor Teeth all the faster if we press on."

"What happens when we get there?" Yoder asked, feeling his looming fate coming closer with every dune they crossed upon. Leeni brushed her hands through her wild hair, paying close attention in case The Wizard finally chose to explain.

He did not, casually replying "All will be revealed within the caverns." much to the teenagers' chagrin.

Leeni huffed. "You say that, but it's important to know something about what we need to deal with. Besides, Yoder deserves to know." She said, admonishing The Wizard's elusive answers.

"Yeah! I'm the hero, I need to know!" Yoder called out, plodding along as fast as his fat feet could carry him in the loose soil. "How am I supposed to save the world? Is there a monster I have to kill?"

Yoder would've kept going if The Wizard didn't inhale heavily, audibly so, like he was about to divulge the secrets of the mission ahead of them. "I will tell you when you need to know, boy!" His tone was authoritative and annoyed. Leeni glared at him, while Yoder closed his dry mouth and looked down at his boots digging gently into the ground every time he stepped forward. Once again, he felt small and incapable, but he refused to give in.

"I'm going home." Yoder said, coming to a stop in the dead, gray dune and dropping the axe into its soft surface. Sixer stalled; weighted foot thrown forward but not cranking to pull his spheroid mass forward. His blue lights fixed on Yoder, watching the boy summon his courage.

Leeni stopped too, her eyes wide. She felt a conflict rise in her that she wasn't prepared for. If Yoder quit now, could the rest of them complete the mission? She did not know and part of her didn't care. What truly frightened her was that deep down, she wanted to go with him. The promise she'd made, to protect him, loomed in her mind and the two times she'd been in danger; he had saved her instead. She turned, looking down at the dusty ground then over at The Wizard who continued to march forward.

"Bye then." Yoder replied to The Wizard's back, turning away from Leeni and him. Sixer hummed deep in his core, turning his head sphere back and forth between the Maker and his friend.

Unseen by the others, The Wizard's face wore a frown. A deep one that turned his eyes into dark shadows and made his angular features seem drawn and weary. He swung around finally, holding his cane down by his hip and called out. "I don't know!"

Yoder turned back, a mixture of concern and confusion cluttering his face. "What do you mean you don't know?" he asked incredulously.

The Wizard stuffed a hand into his coat pocket and began to pull a smaller backup tent from within. There was nothing else he could do save to prepare for another night's rest and a very awkward discussion.

"Sixer, would you mind assisting Miss Leeni with the tent? We'll camp here for a few hours and then make the rest of the trek through the night, I suppose."

Sixer regarded the maker. "Affirmative." It replied and cranked his mass along the tube-like limb attached to his forward flung foot-weight to bring himself closer.

Leeni sighed, moving near The Wizard as well. "Why do we have to set up the tent?" She asked indignantly, but she was put in her place when The Wizard regarded her with sad eyes.

"Yoder and I must talk, if he chooses to explain when we return then he will tell you himself."

Leeni looked at Yoder, who met her eyes and smiled. "Don't worry. I'll tell you everything."

The girl blushed, turning away quickly to hide the redness of her pale cheeks. "Drink some water!" she called, busying herself with unrolling the tent to avoid Yoder's gaze. Yoder didn't seem to understand, looking quite confused as The Wizard approached him and held out the unending waterskin.

The Wizard's Mistake

"She's right, you need to hydrate. Come." The Wizard bid the boy, passing him by to go back up the dune they'd come down from for some privacy. Yoder glanced back at Sixer and Leeni, unstopping the skin, then took a deep, long drink of it before he followed his guide to the dune's peak.

"So…" Yoder said, opening up the conversation.

The Wizard reached into his breast pocket, pulling the scroll that he'd referred to many times before from its impossible depths. He held it out to Yoder. "This is what sent me to you. Look at it," he instructed, while Yoder eagerly unrolled the parchment. He stared at it, unblinking for a long moment before his blue eyes lifted to peer at The Wizard with great incredulity.

"You're serious?" he asked, disbelieving.

The Wizard shrugged, nodding his head once. "That is the prophetic scroll."

Yoder looked back down at it, the broad and aged parchment unrolled and held between two hands while the waterskin leaked endlessly into the sand from under his arm. Written upon the large scroll in glowing, golden script was "A boy of Mater's Range, under the sun at high noon. Only he can save us all." That was it. It said nothing about Yoder specifically, no epic rhyme about him or his legendary dad or his cozy house or what he must do. Just…. He can save us all.

"How?!" Yoder scowled, shaking the scroll. "Stupid magic paper, tell me what to do!"

Perrixstar laughed on Yoder's head. "Silly Fat Slave, paper doesn't have smarts. It's paper!" The faerie dragon giggled, but Yoder was not amused. He scowled more at The Wizard, not rolling the scroll but bunching it awkwardly in his meaty fist.

"You told me that I was chosen! YOU TOLD ME IT WAS MY DESTINY!!" Anger filled the lad, shaking the scroll in The Wizard's face, who put up his hand and cane defensively.

"Well, I calculated the trajectory of the sun's arc in the sky and at high noon, your house would have been under the sun directly. It seemed the most logical reasoning that you would be the one."

"But you don't know that!" Yoder cried, tears forming in his eyes. He'd gone along with all of this insanity because The Wizard had told him of a grand adventure and his great legend, but there was no legend. No great prophecy. "You…ASSHOLE." Yoder snapped, wanting nothing more than to beat The Wizard with his stupid scroll. "I trusted you!"

The Wizard shook his head. "Look at it! It doesn't say you're not the hero," he said, trying to placate the angry youth, but Yoder would have none of that.

"It doesn't say I am, either! There's like…. thirty boys in Mater's Range, you idiot! God, Almighty!" Yoder threw the scroll down, swinging his hands up in defeat. "I'm done. I'm going bloody home!"

The Wizard sighed wearily. "Yoder." He began, pushing his cane into the dune till it stood on his own. "Listen to me, please." The boy stood; hands balled into tight, thick fists at his side. He was angry, hurt, betrayed and it showed on his round face.

"A long, long time ago. God gave all of humanity his only son. One boy, grown into a man, to save the world. He did this with open kindness, charity, and faith but his faith was tested over and over again throughout the journey of his son's young life. The journal of his quest lies in the library of the Mirrored Circle and though it is beyond ancient, what little we mages can decipher states that he went to his death in horrible pain and called to God not to save him but to forgive those who murdered him. Those humans who saw him dead replied that if he were the son of God then let God save him from death. Those humans had no faith, but the son of God did. His path was not laid before him."

Yoder listened, not understanding what The Wizard was trying to say but the story held his attention. The Wizard pulled his short, brimmed hat from his head and ran his fingers through his hair. "What I'm saying is this, I took this mission on faith. As a mage of the circle and as a man of God. Those two sentences on that scroll were all I needed to know, I did the math, and I came to you." He reached out, placing a hand on Yoder's armored shoulder. "My faith was tested, I admit it. I failed you. I dragged you along, kept you in the dark and hoped that my faith…" His other hand was placed on his chest while Yoder watched him with wide eyes. "…would see us through. But you, my boy; you had faith in me, and your faith was false. I lied to you and I'm sorry."

Those words stunned Yoder, his jaw loosening to hang open. He didn't know what to say to the man who'd misled him, taken him away from his home. The Wizard gave his shoulder a gentle squeeze.

"Consistently, throughout this entire mad journey, you followed me, you made choices that frankly surprised me. Caring for Perrixstar…" The Wizard motioned to the small dragon on Yoder's head, who lifted its tiny, scaled head and tipped it to the side.

"Fat Slave is a good slave." It giggled in its twinkling, wind-chime way. Yoder smiled, feeling his cheeks turn hot.

The Wizard chuckled. "Caring about Leeni over there." His hand waved back toward the tent the girl and machine had erected while Yoder looked on, both preparing a small fire somehow. Yoder was very fond of Leeni, and she had been constantly mean to him, but despite all that; he still appreciated her for walking beside him.

"And Sixer. Who do you know back home that befriended an ancient intelligent machine from Solaria?" The Wizard asked with a smile. "In these short days, following a daft man on an even more daft quest for the safety of all mankind; you have done incredible things. More things than I expected of you. I… underestimated you, Yoder Hals." Yoder's head swung back so fast; he nearly gave himself whiplash.

The Wizard smiled more. "From now on, to the end of this insane adventure, you make the decisions. I will only advise and follow your lead. All the might and magic I have, given by God, is at your command."

Flummoxed, that is to say speechless, Yoder tried to speak but only a squeak came out of his mouth. He closed it, took a deep breath to gather his frantic thoughts up and finally found his voice again. "But I don't know what I'm doing…," he said worriedly, a tremble in his voice.

The Wizard shook his head, taking his hand off the boy's shoulder. "Yes, you do. Believe. In yourself, in your friends, and in the will of God. You will find your way. Take some time, think it through. If you want to turn back, we turn back."

As The Wizard pulled his cane from the sand and started down the dune, Yoder stood there and stared across the desolate landscape of Kurn. Mound after mound of dusty nothingness across the horizon, as far as the eye can see. He bent down, struggling to sit in the shifting dirt but once his rump was settled; he exhaled.

"What do I do?" The lad said and thinking that he was speaking to it, Perrixstar replied from above him.

"Save the world. Yes?"

Yoder blinked twice, peering up. "Can you come down from my head, please?" he asked softly, feeling lost and very afraid. Perrixstar arched its back, shimmering wings unfolding so it could hop off Yoder's blonde head and float down to the dust. It padded around like a cat looking for a good spot.

Yoder stared down at the creature as it planted its rump and raised its long neck, so its head was held high, regal. It stared back at him with illuminated purple reptile eyes. "Perri, that's impossible! I don't know what to do." Yoder said, putting his fat hands upon his face and rubbing furiously.

Perrixstar flared its wings then folded them. "Save the world." It repeated.

Yoder groaned. "I know that! But how? The Wizard doesn't know and now he's leaving it up to me! I'm just a boy!" His eyes burned, wet with tears behind his palms.

The Faerie Dragon tipped its head to the side. "You're my slave. You do what I say." It replied.

Yoder laughed despite his sadness, lowering his hands from his teary eyes. "It's that simple, huh?" he asked, watching the small dragon's head nod firmly.

"It is. Save the world, slave." It said firmly. Yoder smiled, wiping his eyes with his fingers while heaving a deep sigh.

"But what if I fail?" he asked, looking to the tiny beast for comfort.

Perrixstar hissed. "I will whip you with my tail. You will not fail, fat slave. I won't let you."

Yoder smiled more. "Can you stop calling me that?"

Perrixstar's reptilian gaze did not falter or blink. "Why?" It asked.

Yoder sniffled, wiping his cheeks. "Because it's mean. I'm not your slave, I'm your friend."

Perrixstar flicked its long tongue out, tasting the dry, acrid air then opened its maw of sharp, vicious teeth in a yawn. Once that wicked mouth closed, it shook out the scales over its head.

"Are you?" It asked finally, drawing a surprised look from Yoder.

"Of course, I am. I've carried you on my head for days now. I fed you and you protected me from that knight. That's what friends do. They help each other."

The small dragon blinked its bright eyes, but Yoder could not decipher what the wild creature was thinking. He waited, wondering what it would say. Perrixstar finally spoke and Yoder's head lifted as soon as its twinkling voice rose in the silence.

"We are friends now." It announced. "And you are friends with everyone, so you will help them and save the world."

Yoder grinned, nodding. "That's what friends do. You're right." He paused, tilting his head. "Can I pet you?" the boy asked with a hopeful tone to his voice.

Perrixstar hissed. "No. I'm not a pet. I'm your friend."

Yoder laughed softly, holding out a hand. "Then can I shake your hand?"

Perrixstar's neck extended, head rearing back. "I have no hands. Why is your hand shaking?"

Yoder continued to laugh. "It's a greeting between human friends. We shake each other's…. paw. Can I shake your paw?" He asked again, to which the small dragon took a moment to mull over before lifting a front claw of tiny, sharp talons.

"Very well."

Yoder smiled, curling his thick hand around the talons and scales very carefully then bobbing them up and down. "Thanks."

When Yoder let go of Perrixstar's claw, the tiny dragon unfurled its butterfly-like wings and beat them to lift itself aloft. Yoder watched, expecting the tiny dragon to fly up onto his head again. It hovered closer, then reared its head back and thrust it forward to thwack the thick top of its head against Yoder's forehead. Yoder flailed, jerking his head back.

"Ow! What'd you do that for?!" He cried out, rubbing the spot where the creature's skull connected with his.

Perrixstar giggled. "This is how dragons greet each other as friends." It explained, tilting to its right while its wings lifted it higher. The Faerie Dragon swooped in a tight arc to land on Yoder's left shoulder instead of the top of his head while Yoder grasped the concept and a silly smile appeared on his jowled face.

"Let's go back to the others." The boy said, feeling much better now. He put a hand in the dusty, dry dune and pushed down until he got some support to heave his bulk up. Perrixstar's claws gripped his armor to stay on his shoulder while the lad got his boots under him and stood up. The two descended from the dune, one riding the other as usual but this time; as friends on a mission.

Leeni had stolen constant glances at the boy on the dune hill while she helped unpack food from The Wizard's basket when the strange man had returned. Sixer settled down on his weighted foot-plates to watch. She was worried about him, but too proud to admit it so it was no surprise that she smiled when she saw him and Perrixstar coming toward the encampment. The Wizard puffed on his long, curved pipe, sitting on the gray ground in front of the tent beside its flap.

Yoder approached the axe he'd left lying on the ground, bending down to lift it in his left hand. He carried it with him low in his hand. All eyes and two blue lights now rested on the boy marching toward them, though The Wizard lofted a brow as well. Yoder stood before his friends and looked from one to the other. Sixer, the lost machine. Leeni, the girl who had his back and helped him learn so many things about himself and the world around him. Finally, The Wizard; the man who started it all.

Yoder took a deep breath, finding his voice and determination. "We go on, if you're with me. I can't turn back now." He announced, holding his head up high.

The Wizard chuckled softly, nodding once to the boy who had grown into a young man in so short a time. "Good lad." He said.

Leeni smiled, standing up and cocking out one hip with her hands coming to rest on the handles of each of her blades. "Let's do this."

Sixer's head-sphere rotated slightly, blue lights focusing on Yoder and one of his arm tubes flexed upward to lift that massive metal mitt on the end. It set to the crab shell shape on top of its head-sphere, affecting a formal salute.

"I am prepared to assist you, Comrade. We will safeguard the maker's race, together." And last but not least, Perrixstar flexed its wings out on Yoder's shoulder. One wing fanned behind Yoder's head and the Faerie Dragon extended its neck.

"For friends!" It said.

The Wizard's greatest mistake smiled at all of his friends, patting his belly with his free hand. "But first, we eat…"

Chapter Thirteen:
Oh God, We're all gonna die!

With bellies full, save for Sixer who had no need for meat or fruit, Yoder Hals and his companions had packed up the tent which The Wizard secreted away in his magical pocket once more. Sharing the waterskin that never emptied to keep hydrated, the five continued their trek across the empty dunes of Kurn toward the terrifying peaks of the Razor Teeth of Levistrax. The end of their adventure, for better or worse, loomed before them like the jagged white maw it was named for.

The closer he got to the mountain's range; the more Yoder worried about the end of his journey. At first, he fretted over the mystery of what he must do but after a few hours of marching through the early morning; he began to wonder what life would be like if he survived this whole, insane ordeal. Would the group go their separate ways? Would he never see Leeni or The Wizard ever again when it was all said and done? He smiled to himself as he thought about never actually earning the golden armor he had once dreamed about, for the breastplate and chainmail, the wolf's head shield and wolf's run sword, all he had acquired were more familiar and welcomed than any gleaming plate mail.

Leeni came to Yoder's side, binding her hair back into a tail with a strip of brown leather. Yoder offered her a nod but said nothing. He still didn't understand the girl, but they had shared dangers and lived through them. Without comprehending her, Yoder believed in her. Shifting the axe handle in his right hand, the boy kept his pace and more importantly, kept his mouth shut. As The Wizard once told him, be patient and let her decide.

The brown-haired girl adjusted her ponytail, short wisping strands of sunny blonde amidst the brown refusing to stay within the bundle. She tightened the leather band's knot a little more then lowered her hands to the handles of her weapons again. "Whatever happens. I'm with you, as promised." She said almost timidly, trying to control the redness creeping onto her cheeks by staring straight ahead.

Yoder felt his pulse quicken, his mind fluttered through a thousand thoughts ranging from fantastical nonsense to dramatic bravado, but the corpulent boy had never been good with words around women and The Wizard's advice circled all his worst impulses.

"Thanks." he said finally, torn but smiling. "Listen, about…. before. I'm sorry. We never got to talk about it. I shouldn't have done that. Kissed you, I mean." When she looked at him directly, Yoder flinched. "You're not going to hit me again, are you?" he asked, looking as pitiful as he felt.

"No," she replied, shaking her head. "You're right though, you shouldn't have but I overreacted so I'm sorry too. I want to be a great adventurer, Yoder. I joined party after party, trying to prove that I can do it. I think I just...started to believe that I couldn't, because no one let me fight with them. I did the chores." She admitted, her expression turning sour and angry. "It's not fair. I know how to fight; I can do it and when I met you; I thought you were my chance to prove it and you were dumb enough to let me." Yoder laughed nervously, he didn't like being told he was dumb, and it showed on his face.

"You can be a jerk sometimes, but you're really not so bad deep down." Leeni continued, looking ahead to help focus her thoughts. "You've saved my life twice now, even though your life's more important."

Yoder scoffed, shaking his head. "No, it's not. I don't even know if I can complete this stupid quest, but I'm gonna try because if I don't…. we're doomed."

"What do you mean?" Leeni asked, confused and looking to the boy for answers. Yoder shrugged, bobbing Perrixstar on his shoulder who answered.

"Wizard Sla…." It corrected itself with a giggle when Yoder squinted at it. "Wizard friend believes that Yoder is the chosen one, but Wizard friend's prophecy doesn't say that. It just says that a boy will save the world. Yoder is a boy; he will save the world." The Faerie Dragon nodded its tiny, scaled head firmly.

Yoder chuckled and said. "Yeah, that."

Leeni's face contorted into a frown, mulling over the news and reasoning that this must have been the conversation last night. "So that's what you two were arguing about." She said finally.

Yoder looked down at the dead soil beneath his boots. "Yeah. But it doesn't matter. The world needs saving and we're already here, so I'm going to do whatever it takes." He spoke with determination. "But I'm glad you're with me." Yoder added afterwards, a little less courageous and more timid.

"We are all with you, Yoder Hals." Sixer's voice echoed tinnily behind the two, prompting Yoder and Leeni to exchange wide eyed glances at being overheard by the machine. He was gently lobbing his foot plates to keep pace at the back of the line without crushing any of his friends under them, but his auditory sensors were quite keen all the same.

Perrixstar hissed at him. "Sixer is a slave, yes? Slave of Solarians, all dead. I will be Sixer Slave's new master." The little beast announced.

Sixer's blue lights shrank and widened, processing the words before he replied. "I am not a slave. I am an autonomous worker drone."

"Drone is slave." Perrixstar replied evenly, turning to sit backwards on Yoder's shoulder so it could stare at the giant spheroid pulling itself from one foot weight to another.

"A drone is not a slave. A drone is…." Sixer stopped speaking, humming low and resonantly for a while. Yoder and Leeni slowed, turning to look back at Sixer to make sure he was alright. Sixer sat on his foot plate, humming for a few more moments. "There is a logical fallacy in my definition. Maker, please explain. Is a drone a slave?"

All eyes turned on The Wizard ahead of the group, who heard the request and stopped short in the gray dust. "Ah, well. Technically, yes. Etymologically, a drone in a colony of bees serves no purpose other than reproducing with the queen bee. In the historical texts of time pre-Solaria, drone was also the term for a magical flying machine that carried out functions remotely commanded by a mage and a derogatory term for a human who does not think for themselves but follows a blind ideology or individual's perspective."

Sixer's blue lights narrowed. "I do not want to be mindless. I am an intelligent construct." It answered a question no one asked.

The Wizard smiled. "So, perhaps you should not refer to yourself as a drone then, eh?" He said, twisting on a booted heel in the loose, dead earth to start onward again.

Yoder nodded. "Why don't you tell us about your life in Solaria?" he asked, beckoning with a hand to get the machine moving again.

Leeni agreed. "Yeah, then we can help you decide what to call yourself." She added, while Perrixstar shook out its wings and announced.

"We know what to call it. My New Slave."

All of them ignored the tiny dragon. Sixer hummed a while, processing and then finally began the tale. It seemed the most logical course as defined by the alliance of people he traveled with.

"I am not alive. I was manufactured by the Makers to gather materials and make repairs to the infrastructure of Solaria City." He began, but Yoder cut him off by turning back.

"Wait. Sixer. You -are- alive. You have thoughts and you make your own decisions," he said.

Sixer responded tinnily. "Inconclusive. I am a machine. An intelligent construct is not alive."

Yoder shrugged. "Well, I think you're alive," he said.

Sixer did not respond beyond a simple "Thank you" to that. He could not process perspective, only information. After a short silence walking down the next dune, Yoder glanced back at the giant machine.

"If you're an intelligent construct, whatever that means, do you have ideas? Like….do you look at a broken table and know how to fix it or do you think "that should go there" and do it?" he asked.

Sixer responded instantly. "I am programmed with a database of schematics, I use my optical sensors to determine the object: Table, the type, and then my processing unit searches through the database for the appropriate diagram."

"That's kind of like a memory, I guess," Yoder mentioned, scratching his stubbly chins.

Leeni giggled. "Not really." Yoder huffed at her, which only made her giggle more. "It's not! He didn't memorize those schematics. He's had them. Right?" She asked the machine, which nodded its head-sphere.

"Correct. I have always had these schematics within my database." It resonated in reply.

Yoder shrugged, jostling Perrixstar on his shoulder. "I say it counts," he muttered.

Sixer hummed, finally emitting that tinny, resonant echo of a voice from its main sphere. "All workers of Solaria were programmed with linguistics, analytics, the database of knowledge, and social order."

Yoder exchanged glances with Leeni. "I don't know what those words mean," Yoder said, the girl nodding as well. Sixer's blue lights whirred, moving from one to the other.

"Linguistics is the study of language, speaking. It is how I was able to determine the best way to communicate with you, Yoder." The boy made an 'oh' face, and Sixer continued to explain.

"Analytics is a system of processing data, a form of thinking." It hummed, launching a foot-plate forward and then cranking the pulley of its leg tube to drag itself forward. "I have explained the database of knowledge, so social order is the totality of interrelationships within a society. It dictates where us, the worker units, are within the hierarchy of Solaria as well as all citizens of the kingdom." Leeni and Yoder exchanged confused glances. The Wizard chuckled ahead of them.

"What he means is that if everyone knows who is in charge, then everyone knows the social order."

"Ohhhhh." Yoder began to nod as if he understood, but Leeni giggled and shoved his shield arm.

"You have no clue what they're talking about, do you?"

Yoder laughed, shaking his head. "Not one word." The boy replied. While the two teenagers shared amusement, Sixer watched them without understanding.

"Social order is integral to the survival of any society. Solaria's social order preserved the natural history and culture of the entire kingdom. We, the working-class automatons, comprise the backbone of Solaria's social order. We construct, repair, and bolster the infrastructure of the kingdom so that the Makers may see to the culture and magic without impediment."

"Impediment?" Yoder asked, brows furrowing, and his head tilted slightly like a dog when spoken to.

Sixer hummed, responding tinnily. "Obstacle. Each of us contributes to the whole, as dictated by the Grand Magistrar. Food is equally shared amongst the Makers as tended by constructs designed for farming, for example."

The Wizard chuckled softly. "Ah yes, I read about this. Social Communism, where the governance oversees and equitably distributes the fruits of labor and industry amongst the entire civilization. It's an archaic form of rule that Solaria thought best suited the old world's needs."

Yoder frowned. "But what do you get out of it, Sixer?" he asked curiously, but with concern in his tone.

"The Makers were given food. You fixed and built their homes and things, so what do you get in return?" Sixer replied instantly. "We, the working class, are given shelter and upgrades to make us more efficient as the Makers designed them."

Yoder looked to Leeni, who hadn't quite caught on yet, and marched forward with a dismayed but unsure expression on her face. Yoder stopped walking and turned around.

"Sixer, I don't understand. You were built to provide for the Makers and were given nothing but upgrades and shelter? Can't you do those things yourself?"

The Wizard stumbled a step; Yoder's naively pointed question surprised him. He caught himself with his cane, recovering quickly, and chose not to speak on that altogether. He'd read the histories, what few archives remained after Solaria was lost to time, but he wanted to see how the boy handled this odd exchange.

Sixer, on the other hand, resonated with a reply. "Correct. I am capable of self-repair, constructing any object within the database of knowledge, including the upgrades cataloged there in order to better aid my kind."

Yoder looked up at the machine with wide, blue eyes. "Then why did you have to work for the Makers?"

A light switched on in Leeni's eyes then, finally seeing what Yoder was questioning and she took a sudden gasp of breath. Her left hand lifted off her sword's handle, touching her mouth when Sixer answered the young man.

"So that the Makers might progress themselves, designing new magic and science to make the whole of the world safer and better." It stated, straight from its programming code.

Yoder frowned, looking back at Leeni, who met his gaze with sadness in hers. She understood now. The Automaton Class were…. slaves.

The Wizard had stayed silent till this point, but he could feel the tension heavily in the air now and cleared his throat. "Solaria is gone. Sixer may do as Sixer pleases now; you know. There's no sense in mulling over the societal structure of a dead civilization. We must look forward," he said, then glanced back to find both teens looking at each other. "No, seriously. I mean it. Look forward." The Wizard added, drawing both Leeni and Yoder's gaze ahead. There before them stood the jagged walls of stone that comprised the Razor's Teeth of Levistrax only a Solarian mile away.

Yoder's lips pursed tightly, putting aside the past of his new friend and companion. Leeni took her hand down from her face and reached out to lay it on the smooth, metal border of Yoder's shield like she meant to touch his arm but couldn't.

"Are you ready?" she asked softly, trying to ignore the implication that the greatest society of history had made slaves in favor of the impending doom before them.

Yoder swallowed that lump in his throat, nodding firmly. "I think so." He said with a dry mouth.

The girl smiled reassuringly. "Any thoughts then?" She asked gently, to which Yoder closed his mouth, began to chuckle sardonically, then replied.

"Oh God, Oh God. We're all going to die!"

The Wizard laughed sharply. "Well then, let's get on with it!" He added with forced cheer, twirling his cane between his fingers. "Victory or Death, as they say. This is where it all begins to end, my friends."

Leeni scoffed. "Helpful, you're not." She snapped, but Yoder shook off his doubt and fear as he'd learned to do these last days of the journey.

"Right." A firm nod, marching forward a little faster now. "This is it. Whatever's in there, we must win." He said with conviction.

The Wizard replied. "Ohh, we call them gnolls. You know, some mages of the circle even believe they're evolved humans...or rather devolved humans. Gnarly, ugly things with primitive brains from surviving in the dark for too long."

Yoder thought he was doing well until The Wizard explained. Somehow, the unknown was less frightening than the known and his mind conjured up horrifying images of all manner of disgusting creatures now thanks to his guide. "She's right, you're not helping!" Yoder barked, which Leeni giggled at and caught up to Yoder's side.

"We'll be fine. I promise." She said to him, trying to soothe his fear.

Yoder nodded. "Yeah, we'll be fine. What's evolve mean?"

The Wizard rolled his eyes. "Nevermind that. Just know that gnolls are vicious things and keep your wits about you." He snapped but stopped so suddenly that Yoder almost marched right by him. The lad turned, dragging his shield out from under Leeni's touch to do so and regarded The Wizard with confusion.

"What? What's wrong?"

The Wizard turned away and looked up at Sixer. "You can alter your mass, correct? Change shape?"

Sixer hummed, coming to a stop on his forward most footplate. "Correct." It echoed a reply.

"Good. You'd be best served in a smaller capacity, I think. We know not how large the caverns will be." The Wizard stated.

"Acknowledged." Sixer said. Its massive spheroid shape shuddered and the sound of gears cranking rose. Its arm and leg tubes retracted into the central sphere as much as they could before the plating separated and began to move in succession inward. Each rounded plate that comprised the sphere grinded against the other in a horrifying series of high-pitched sounds that made everyone, even Perrixstar wince. The noise became so terrible that Yoder closed his eyes in some vain effort to block out the sonic anguish until it was stopped. It stopped so suddenly that he didn't realize it was over at first.

When the young man opened his blue eyes, he stared at a smaller but no less impressively statured Sixer. Now only eight stone high, his form appeared almost like a knight in armor rather than a round colossus. The curved plates conformed into leg guards at the front and back of his foot weights and similarly greaves over the arm tubes. Two plate edges jutted from the top parallel to his head-sphere and crab shell covering resembling tall pauldrons and the center mass while shrunken, still was rounded in a way that reminded Leeni of Yoder's belly under his breastplate.

"Excellent." The Wizard remarked, unbothered. He turned around and continued to walk onward, closer to the base of the mountain nearest the troupe. Yoder and Leeni stared as Sixer loped by, foot-weights now acting more like feet.

"Wow...," said Yoder, amazed. Leeni smiled at him then Sixer, bouncing on her booted feet to catch up to The Wizard ahead of them again.

Chapter Fourteen:
Did you see that?

The wide-mouthed cavern they found in the rock face of the mountain was so dark, thanks to Kurn's heavy dust which clouded the sky above, that The Wizard was forced to pause at the opening and cast spells of light. One upon Yoder's shield, the wolf's head now glowing brilliantly. The other was cast on Perrixstar's tail, who found the glowing appendage more than amusing and refused to stop waving it about behind Yoder's head. Still, it was effective in illuminating the area behind the boy.

The final casting was done on the crystal head of The Wizard's cane, because Sixer's glowing blue eye-lights saw in spectrums that humans could not and he, therefore, didn't need light to operate. With everyone now prepared, each snacked upon a bit of fruit or a strip of dried meat except the machine before they began to enter the dreaded end of their journey. Yoder went first, shield at the ready and sword while the axe was tucked into his belt. The blade rested atop the shield, which showed white light ahead of them like a flashlight in the hands of a group of teenage sleuths.

The Wizard walked behind Yoder at his left arm, holding his cane aloft above him which was aided by Perrixstar's wobbling tail on Yoder's right shoulder near where Leeni Vex stalked with both sword and dirk in hand to cover the boy's right flank. Sixer loomed over them all at the rear, lumbering loudly with foot-weights thumping off the stone ground. The hope was that such a calamity might frighten the beasts of the dark places away from them and at the very least, make more intelligent creatures think twice about mounting an attack.

It was a slow pace, but one that shared safety among them all. Each too concerned about the shadows where their lights did not reach to speak much if at all, their eyes wide and alert save for Perrixstar's which never really dilated to begin with. Unfortunately for them, the inhabitants of this mountain were born and raised, age after age, in deep darkness and had no trouble seeing through the murky black. However, they were a primitive lot and the blinding shines that emanated from the exploring group kept them at bay for now. Fearful, misunderstanding, and keeping to the shadows just beyond the painful brilliance.

In the dark, they moved. Creeping between outcroppings and natural spikes in the ground, gnolls crawled and skittered unseen. They had come to witness the noise, finding more than one alien intruding upon their home. Malformed eyes stared through the black that was bright as day to them, huge pupils blinking owlishly to take in details until one of the hellish brights swept their way and forced them back in blinking, silent pain. The brights alone were dangerous, but the aliens carried tools of war as well.

A few of the forward scouts broke off and scampered back into their tunnels, crawling away to bring news of invasion. That was what this was to them. Invasion. Monsters from the beyond come to kill them. These scouts moved quickly on hands and feet, alternating between this beastly lope and walking upright as they were capable of doing. Each weaved through the network of smaller tunnels off the larger caverns and tributaries to return to the warren where their leader awaited them.

It had no name, their leader. No gnoll had a name in the traditional sense beyond the simple 'you'. This was because gnolls no longer had language. In the dark, sound was your enemy. Animals followed sound as much as scent, insects hunted and trapped prey based on sound; so gnolls had developed hand gestures to communicate and only made sounds when they must. Even death was a silent affair in the dark. This was used to signal the leader, a large, hulking gnoll with only one good eye and only half a mouth of decent chewing teeth in his dirty, mangled skull. His muscles were no detriment to him though, which he used to defend his right to lead and his tribe mercilessly.

For that reason, the gnoll chief wore spider fangs around his thick neck, the scales of giant lizards sewn together with sinew upon his chest and shoulders, and a skirt of fur around his middle. Small bones were pierced through the flesh of his face, marking strength and endurance while larger bones were tied to his arms and elbows, even knees. Across his lap as he sat upon the great stone of the warren rested a carved stone axe with shaved bone handle, dyed dark with the blood of slain beasts.

The gnoll chief motioned with strong, but gnarled fingers to his scouts. Each motioned back, one at a time, reporting what they saw of the invasion. Drool pooled in the malformed jaw of the chief; they would eat well when these intruders were killed. He wanted the large lizard for himself, he liked to eat lizard most of all the creatures of the dark. The gnoll chief lifted his axe, clacking the bone tip of its handle upon the great stone to alert all the warren around him. A hundred wide eyes raised to witness the chief who signaled by hand, the call to war.

They would pour from the tunnels and cracks of the stone like blood, destroying the invaders without hesitation, without fear, he signed to his people. The gnoll chief pushed up onto flat, gnarly toed feet and raised his axe high above his head. "HOO-CHAKOO!" He bellowed out of his curled, cleft mouth. The warren roared in unison the same sound, letting it echo through the tunnels and paths back to the intruders so they would know that war was coming.

"What the hell was that?" Leeni asked nervously as the echoing reached them twice, first a single, whisper of a sound so far away that was followed by a much louder, jumbled, echoing roar. The Wizard grimaced. "Gnolls, like I expected. Steady on, eyes alert." He advised, patting Yoder's shoulder with his right hand. The teenager in the lead kept reminding himself not to soil his leathers as he pushed forward, warily over the uneven stone floor of the tunnel.

"And you're absolutely sure whatever I need to do to save the world is in here, right? No room for error? I would really love to run away right now." Yoder said, trying not to sound as terrified as he truly was and failing quite spectacularly at it. "No, no. I'm certain." The Wizard replied, refusing to admit that even he was quaking in his fine boots right now. All the power cosmic he possessed at his command did not give him the confidence that he could take on gnolls and survive.

Ahead of them, in the mouth of the tunnel leading to a larger cavern, Yoder saw something move. "Did you see that?" he asked, leaning forward slightly to peer down the length of his sword which he used without thinking as a targeting sight for the shield's glowing light. "Something moved over there…" He murmured, but his shield was struck with a clack off the light-spelled center and Yoder screamed. Yep, like a little girl. His shield turned down instinctively, sweeping across the dull stone ground before him. "What was that?!" he asked, before something else struck him on the top of his bent head. "OW!" Perrixstar reared back, hissing.

"Stones! Hunker down, all of you!" Called out The Wizard, hunching behind Yoder who raised his shield up again to protect his friends. Leeni did the same as The Wizard, moving behind the boy's bulk while Perrixstar climbed across Yoder's upper back. Sixer hummed, lifting his wide, metal mitts and positioned them both, side by side, above the group. "There are four humanoids throwing stones at us, they are positioned at fifteen degrees northeast, twenty-five degrees northeast, twelve degrees northwest, and twenty-two degrees northwest." It resonated in alert. "What the hell does that mean?!" Cried Yoder, listening to things bounce off his shield from behind it.

"Oh, for God's….it means forward left and forward right! Two on each side!" The Wizard called out from behind the boy. Yoder snapped. "Don't bite my head off about not knowing ancient languages!" He said angrily, pushing forward at a faster pace now. "Sixer, tell me when we're close to the cavern!" The Wizard growled. "It's MATHS, Boy!" Sharpening the word with punctuative anger. "Maths! I told them we should add a standardized educational system but nobody bloody listens to me!"

The huddled mass of adventurers continued forward, following Yoder's lead under the protection of his shield and Sixer's hands.

"Nobody's listening to you now, shut up!" Yoder called back angrily, growing more and more frustrated with the rocks clacking off his shield every moment.

"If you didn't listen, you'd have no idea where they are!" The Wizard hissed right back. "Give me a moment, I'll call the winds!" He added, already tired of this nonsense. "Fine!" He heard Yoder call back.

Once again, The Wizard drew upon the essence of life all around him. The stones gave off the wrong kind of power, but it was power nonetheless and The Wizard could still use it. He began to chant the words again, in the old tongue, while the energy of all matter was drawn into the glowing crystal tip of his cane. He'd need more of it to make a powerful spell; the elemental alignment was all wrong, but The Wizard feared using earth spells that might weaken the mountain itself and crush them all with its collapse.

"Everybody stop!" Yoder called back, holding position since The Wizard stopped to chant. "Protect The Wizard!" The boy called out, shifting to his left to put himself more fully in front of the man. Leeni moved too, but it was Sixer who sealed the protective circle by moving behind The Wizard and lowering his wide hands like shields into position before Leeni on one side and the chanting spellcaster with the other.

Yoder swept with his shield, trying to see the gnolls that were attacking them with the brightness of the shield's spell-light only to accidentally blind one. It was hit full-face with the beam of light and its misshapen head recoiled with a cry as its eyes were blinded. "Did you see it?!" Yoder frantically called out, though no one else was looking. The blinded gnoll writhed and thrashed its thin, warped body of sickly, pale limbs covered in the dried flesh of the dead as clothing. Yoder could hardly believe what he was seeing. "My god, they're disgusting!"

The Wizard's chanting grew louder behind him, telling the boy that the spell would be completed soon enough, and he couldn't be more happy to know that. Especially now, when he swept his light back across the cavern opening and found a surge of more twisted people crawling and running toward them with crude weapons swinging wildly over their heads. "Oh no…," he said, stunned by the onslaught's arrival. "We're in trouble!!" Yoder called out fearfully, hoping The Wizard had enough power to handle it all.

The boy hunched down behind his shield, bracing himself as hard as he could in preparation long before the horde was even halfway up the tunnel toward them. Long before The Wizard's spell was even successfully cast. He closed his eyes tight and waited but heard nothing happen. Only the breathing of Leeni and Perrixstar behind him, not to mention the gentle hum of Sixer as well. Time passed on, still nothing occurred as far as he could tell and so, Yoder finally opened his eyes and glanced over his shoulder.

It was then that the spell was finished, The Wizard swung his cane back and over Yoder's head, where the crystal unleashed a wave of gale force down the tunnel. There was no fanfare, no dramatic cry of a word. Just the long incantations end and a somewhat dramatic point. Wind howled like a tornado through the stone corridor, ripping less sturdy rocks from the ground, walls, and ceiling as it roared through. The coming swarm of gnolls were thrown backwards, off their feet, yowling into the loud winds that stole the sound away as surely as it stole their footing and cast them into the far cavern.

"Oh." The Wizard said, pulling his cane back and peering over Yoder's head. "Are there more of them? Damn it all. I would've put more into the spell." He mentioned, surprised.

Yoder peered over his shield, lowering it some as he stood up straight. "Didn't you say there are lots of them in these mountains? Why weren't you expecting more?" he asked, glancing back at The Wizard who pulled his cap from his head and folded it up to tuck into his vest pocket.

"Well, I would assume so, but I figured we'd have more time before we stumbled upon a large nest."

Yoder groaned. "A large nest?! How many are in a nest??" he asked, holding up his sword to press the flat of it to his forehead since he had no more hands to facepalm with.

"Oh, usually forty, fifty. Some of them can get up close to the hundreds, but I doubt that's the case here. I'm sure I handled the majority of them." The Wizard replied with a shrug as the Chief stepped up into the mouth of the tunnel from the cavern. He seethed spittle through his crooked lips, pounding his axe handle on the heavy stone floor.

"HOO-CHAKOO!!" he bellowed once more, gnolls surging around him to rush at the group.

Startled, Yoder jumped at the booming war-cry and backed into The Wizard while raising his shield. He felt a hand push on his head.

"The fight's that way, lad," said The Wizard, moving to Yoder's left with his cane at the ready before him. "No time for large spells, we're in for it now!"

Yoder put a foot forward then, seeing the oncoming sea of shadowed figures coming their way and his brain went stupid as it often does in these situations. "Forty to a hundred?!" he cried out in exasperation, looking back to the Wizard who had moved to the other side of him. Yoder blinked, began to turn his head the other way when Leeni shouted. "Look out!"

Yoder raised his shield just in time for something to slam into it, shocking him out of his stupidity. He saw the girl rush forward, a spray of warm liquid splashed across his face, and he instantly knew what it was. Blood. Just like back at the Gates of Kurn, it was warm and viscous. "Leeni!" he called out, pushing forward with his shield in four steps before he hit something, and instinct took over. His sword surged forward in his hand, overtop the shield to sink into something that made a guttural cry. It was a battle once again, for survival, for the mission.

The boy clenched his jaw, lowering his shield enough to see over as he waded into the first line of monstrous men. He wasn't as frightened as before, but fear still kept his mind sharply focused on the moment as he blocked a small, stone axe swung toward him and replied to it with a sharp thrust of the Wolf's Run sword. They came at him from every direction but behind, slashing with small rough knives and axes, bashing at his Wolf's Head shield with hammer stones and simple clubs. He found a strange rhythm in it all, moving his shield back and forth to defend against the raining blows and stabbed where he could in between.

It was Leeni who responded the best to the conflict, dancing through the spaces between misshapen men with her gleaming blades. She cut across a middle here, slashed a thigh there, reversed her circle and cut an arm near off with her short blade while her dirk drank deeply of a neck when she punched by the owner's failed attempt to duck back. The girl was driven back by three, moving to Yoder's side and he began to deflect their attacks while she twirled around behind him and came back to the fight on the other side, cutting and slicing. The Wizard moved far to the wall, holding his cane in both hands at his side. He was chanting, a rapid version of the wind spell that released small bursts of air from the crystal tip which he aimed at gnoll after gnoll to knock them off their feet.

The construct had begun to march to the right of Leeni's starting point, though he quickly lost sight of the girl in the wave of wild, small bodies that he slapped away with his giant metal hands. His mass cranked, extending arms and legs as much as he could and he kicked a footplate out into one mutated gnoll, crushing it. On his way toward that plate, Sixer's hands swung like yo-yos at the end of their strings, whirling around and around to smack down anything in their path. Gnolls and rocks, mostly, pulverized by the velocity and weighted hands while weighted feet crushed anything they landed upon.

The second wave of gnolls hit a team in stride, blindly rushing into Sixer's whirling limbs to slow the giant machine's momentum and try to overwhelm him. A gnoll managed to grab Yoder's shield, pulling on it as hard as it could only to receive the bite of his sword rather than success. Yoder plunged the blade deep in its chest with a cry of brutality but couldn't pull it free enough to stop a club being swung at his face. He blinked at the last second, wincing but heard the clang of stone off metal and his eyes shot wide open again. The clubbing gnoll was kicked back by Leeni after she deflected the blow, parried a knife's cut with her dirk and slashed the gnoll with the club down its middle. It screeched then fell dead, leaving Leeni to swing her short blade up again and make some room.

"Finally!" He heard the girl call out. "I only owe you one now!"

Chapter Fifteen:
Like dying in a dream

The Gnoll Chief motioned to his tribe for the first and second waves of attack, but his lust for blood and meat got the better of him by then. The giant gnoll, strongest among them, surged forward amidst the rest with his axe gripped tightly and as the third wave engaged the invaders; he picked his target as the strongest among them. The female had killed most of his people so far. He did not understand magic, only death and so he marked her as the champion among the intruders.

Sixer battered gnolls who came too close to his whirling limbs, constantly pushing at a slow pace forward over the bodies he knocked to the stone floor. He showed no signs of stopping, no matter how hard the gnolls tried to weigh him down with body after body. A ceaseless machine grinding mutated men under his endless gears.

The Wizard, however, was growing bored with his quick casting and had taken to moving from left to right behind the others while sending blast after blast of wind power from his crystal tipped cane to any gnoll before him. He found new and interesting ways to speak the cantrip that activated the spell, the very end of an amazing litany that would blow them all clear out the back of the mountain if he had enough time and energy to do so.

So instead, The Wizard continued his strafing movement and fired volley after volley each accentuated by a different tone of voice to speak the words. "Princips ventus!" He'd announce, followed by "Princips ventus?". Another round, he'd speak it quickly and the next time; he'd speak it slow. Sometimes, he even spoke it higher pitched and low to make a sort of game of it. It was all so very boring to the man who could summon lightning and storms of fire. How he wished they'd just get on with it.

While Leeni moved, circling Yoder and his shield with lightning-fast grace and speed, Yoder pushed forward deflecting attacks and making short thrusts where he could, but he was beginning to tire out already. His sword arm ached, his shield arm was going numb from the repeated blows that shook it and the shield attached to it. He didn't know how much more he had in him but to stop meant death, so he couldn't stop. While The Wizard blasted gnoll after gnoll away to help give him breathing room and Sixer kept much of the force busy trying to overwhelm his whirling arms, Leeni continued to slip between gnolls and slice at them with deadly alacrity.

Her short blade dug deep into the side of a gnoll, who curled up reflexively and pitched over in agony. She pulled the sword free and brought it around only for a large hand of gnarly fingers to catch it in palm. Leeni gasped, looking up to see the largest gnoll snarling down at her with a crooked, mangled face full of rage. Her first instinct was to let go of the sword and flee, terror gripping her heart as she watched the huge, crude axe rise high. "LEENI!" She heard Yoder's voice distant but afraid and the battle rushed back to her mind.

The girl twisted, holding the sword still. Her body spun and her arm protested but did not give as she swung the other limb behind the giant gnoll and rammed the curved tip of her blade into its rear end. All fat and meat, but it served her well. The Gnoll Chief roared in pain, the axe slash pulled up short and swung very wide. Leeni grinned, spinning back around so her arm stopped screaming at her and jerking the dirk's tip free of the Gnoll Chief's hindquarters only to return to him in a swing toward his gut. At the same time, she used her momentum to pull on the sword in his grasp.

The great Gnoll howled painfully but saw the arc of the dirk coming back around for his guts and he pulled back defensively. Leeni's short blade cut through his palm as she jerked it free, spilling blood upon the stone below them. Proud of herself, Leeni moved to find better footing but the rage of the large Gnoll propelled him forward and he slammed his larger, harder body into hers. Leeni grunted, thrown backwards to bounce off another gnoll in the throng of the battle. She stumbled forward as the Gnoll Chief swung his axe, barely getting her sword up in time to stop it from chopping her in half.

"LEENI!" screamed Yoder, pushing with his shield and thrusting with his sword as hard as he could to try to get to her as he watched her face the biggest gnoll of the bunch. But no matter how many he knocked down or stabbed, they just kept getting in his way and panic began to get the better of him. Full of fire, but exhausted; Yoder battered a gnoll with his shield but felt a flash of pain up his sword arm as a knife nicked him. He stabbed toward the pain only to feel a solid blow crash into his shield arm's shoulder and Yoder groaned. It was all too much for the boy now.

Then the tunnel lit up, bright as day. From behind Yoder crawled Perrixstar, right up onto his sword-arm's shoulder. Its long neck undulating already, it thrust its tiny head forward and blew the mightiest of flames that it had ever blown before. A gout no hotter than a torch, but just as suddenly bright which the Faerie Dragon whipped around over Yoder's head like a flamethrower. The gnolls overpowering Yoder screamed, falling backward and dropping their weapons to cover their faces. Even the Gnoll Chief was caught by surprise.

Leeni had spared herself from death deflecting the axe blow, but the force of it left her arm shaking. The limb ached from wrist to shoulder, while she tried to recover from the shock of such a powerful strike. When Perrixstar's fire startled the Gnoll Chief, Leeni saw her opening but wasn't sure she had the strength to end it. With a roar, the girl ran forward and put all her weight into the thrust of her short blade aimed just under the large Gnoll's sternum. She felt it sink, thrust her chest against the pommel and pushed with all her body's might to make the sword tip upward.

The Gnoll Chief howled as the sword dug into him, his free hand grabbing for the blade, but the girl shoved down on it and he felt the sword rip through his insides. The result was a guttural sound of confusion, unsure what just happened. A moment later and he looked down at the bloody, small female with her sword in his guts. His mangled, ugly face twisted further in dying rage and he sprayed thick spit as he roared down at her defiantly. The axe was raised high, looking for one last swing before the light left the Gnoll Chief's eyes but Leeni jumped up and raked her dirk's edge across his throat.

Blood poured from the large gnoll's neck, his hand dropped the axe behind him and it hit the stone with a heavy thump just before his body did. Leeni jerked on her sword three times before she could get it free of the fresh corpse and with heaving breaths, turned on the rest of the Gnoll warren remaining. She could barely keep the short sword upright, briefly reminding her of that longsword back at Fletch and Flicker's tavern in Galarion's Hollow. It only made her more determined to hold onto the weapon.

Yoder's blue eyes were wide when Perrixstar began vomiting fire but remained so even after the flames died down and he watched Leeni kill the largest gnoll of the whole lot. ".... Good God," he said, unable to believe his eyes. The brutality of it was amazing, both terrible and wonderfully so. A gnoll rose up in his line of vision and he smashed his shield into its face without thinking, the twisted man knocked back to the ground unconscious. He wasn't the only one in awe.

The rest of the warren watched their chieftain fall dead to the stone. Each one dropped their weapons and ran silently from the tunnel as fast as they could. Those blinded by the Faerie Dragon's flames stumbled over corpses and weapons, banged into each other and stone but tried to flee all the same. Some crawled, some bled out trying to join the rest as the five watched on in stunned confusion.

Yoder stumbled over corpses to reach Leeni, but his arms hurt so much that all he could do was stand at her side with his limbs hanging down uselessly. "That…" He breathed out. "…was…amazing." Finally able to huff the other two words when his burning lungs were full of air. He stopped trying to talk, sweat and gore dripping off his smiling face.

Perrixstar purred. "I know. My flames are more than those ugly humans can handle."

Yoder eyed the small dragon on his shoulder, trying to laugh but only ended up hacking and coughing in a vaguely laughing way. Leeni smiled at him, her tied back hair matted down with so much blood that she was suddenly a redheaded girl instead. Streaks of gnoll ichor ran down her face, dripping off her sloped chin and round cheeks.

"Thanks. Thought I was done for a moment there. It was all Perri, though. She saved us."

Yoder blinked at the girl, sucking in air. "What? She?!" he asked with a wheeze, looking from bloody woman to perched lizard.

Leeni grinned wider. "She kicks ass, she's a girl."

Yoder scowled. "I kicked ass, and I'm a boy. That doesn't make sense."

"Of course, it does," Leeni replied cheekily, rubbing blood off her face with her gloved hand. "You just don't understand women." she added, taking a moment to slide her sword back into its scabbard and then see her dirk nestled in its cradle as well.

Yoder scoffed. "Bloody right, I don't. You're wrong, though. I'll prove it," he said, sheathing his sword as well before he looked up at Perrixstar. "Go on then, tell her," he said to the Faerie Dragon, upnodding and waiting to be proven right.

Perrixstar tilted its head. "I am a dragon, stupid humans."

Yoder huffed. "Yeah but are you a boy dragon or a girl dragon?" he asked more clearly.

Perrixstar hissed. "There are only dragons, Yoder!" It responded angrily.

Yoder's expression eased to regret. "Alright, alright. I'm sorry!" he said to the little creature, then slid a sly smile toward Leeni. "See? Not a girl."

Leeni rolled her eyes. "Just because there aren't boy or girl dragons doesn't change anything I said. Girls kick ass," she finished with a proud grin, moving to stand in that cocky way she adopted often but the lancing pain in her wrist shot up her arm as she put it to her hip. "Ow!" she hissed, giving up on standing tall in order to nurse her arm.

"You're hurt," Yoder said, reaching for the limb she was cradling to her middle now.

"I'll be fine," Leeni said, turning her body away from his touch.

Yoder frowned, nodding. "Well, we know for sure that one girl can kick ass, and that's you. Be careful with that arm, okay?" He said, stepping over a gnoll corpse to go check on The Wizard and Sixer.

Leeni watched him go with a surprised look on her face, one that turned to regret at the way she'd brushed off his aid. Yoder saw none of it as he approached The Wizard, who was nudging corpses off Sixer's foot-weights to free them.

"You alright?" the boy asked.

"Aye, hale and hearty but hoarse of voice. You?" The Wizard responded, looking up.

Sixer turned his blue lights on Yoder, the glowing orbs shrinking smaller. "I am detecting no critical injuries. Comrade Yoder is well," he resonated, which made Yoder smile and nod.

"Yeah, I'm fine. Just exhausted, my arms feel like they're made of sand."

"Good. What of Leeni? She fought that giant Gnoll with incredible skill," The Wizard offered, finding a spot of stone floor that wasn't occupied by a body around Sixer for which to place the foot of his cane.

Yoder shrugged. "She says she's fine, but she's nursing her arm. Too stubborn to let me see it, so we should take care going forward."

Sixer hummed. "I will offer my aid, I have many diagnostics and repair techniques for human injuries in my database of knowledge," he resonated tinnily, starting to squish bodies on his way toward the girl.

The Wizard eyed Yoder critically. "That was a heavy battle, my boy. You weathered it well."

Yoder shrugged casually like it was no big deal, but he was cheering inside, and it showed in his blue eyes. The Wizard chuckled, seeing this. "Though their weapons were crude, their numbers were overwhelming. We should take a brief rest and continue on carefully," he advised, starting to walk over bodies toward Leeni and Sixer.

Yoder nodded his agreement. "I could use a nap, but a chance to catch my breath is just as good. Can I have the waterskin, please?" The Wizard nodded, pausing to fish in his extra-dimensional pocket for it. When found, he passed the skin over to the boy who eagerly began drinking from it.

By the time both had joined Leeni and Sixer, Sixer was using the rod of a broken crude axe and some of the clothing from a dead gnoll to fashion a splint on Leeni's sword arm. "Her wrist is fractured, and she has suffered bruising in her shoulder," he announced to Yoder and The Wizard.

Leeni frowned at Sixer. "I can fight, don't worry about me," she said, frustration and pain lacing her voice.

Yoder shook his head. "Fine, but don't overdo it. Just be careful, okay?" Leeni looked down, but The Wizard caught the red of her cheeks clear enough in the light of his cane's crystal tip.

"We rest for a bit, preferably away from the dead lest some creature of the dark come looking to eat and find us," The Wizard mentioned, moving on.

Yoder offered his shoulder to Leeni's good arm. "Here, hold on till we're out of this tunnel. I don't want you to fall." For once, the girl accepted his help and placed her hand on his shoulder with a quiet, gentle nod.

Sixer crushed everything under his foot-weights as he walked from the tunnel into the cavern and scanned for more gnolls. "We are alone," he said tinnily, hearing and detecting no further dangers at the moment.

Yoder helped Leeni out of the tunnel, then moved forward when she let go so, he could look about the cavern curiously. It was empty, but for the echo of water trickling somewhere amidst the rocks. "There's more than one tunnel ahead. Which one do we take?" he asked The Wizard, looking back.

The Wizard sat down on a rock and folded his legs under him. "You rest and I shall find out," he said, laying his cane across his thighs.

Yoder sat down on a stone, drinking from the waterskin once more. It was always cool, refreshing, and after sweating heavily; it was a welcome feeling. He passed the skin to Leeni when she carefully sat down on the rock beside him. Sixer stood between each stone, one with the two teens and the other bearing The Wizard who had begun to quietly chant to himself.

Leeni drank from the waterskin, lowering it with a pleased sigh. "That really hit the spot." She said, Yoder nodded slowly in agreement.

While the two rested and Sixer stood guard, The Wizard's chant sent three magical projections of himself outward from his body like spirits. Each one coursed through tunnels that crisscrossed and wound around one another. These spirits moved at incredible speed, dictated by The Wizard's will. They soared through caverns and chasms, two winding downward and one winding up into a spiraling chasm with a crude but manmade ledge running the perimeter. The projection flew out into the center of the chasm, looking around with an ethereal twirl.

The Wizard banished the other two, focusing on that one with great curiosity. There was little reason to think that Gnolls had built such an elaborate ledge to walk up, which left him to believe something else had done so. The projection of him started upward, floating higher and higher in the empty chasm that seemed to fill much of the space of the mountain's insides. He saw light at the top, a pinprick of it high above, and his projection began to soar up towards it when a brilliant brightness rose from the center of the ceiling and engulfed the apparition.

The Wizard jolted awake. "Good God!" he cried out, startled and clutching his collar. Yoder and Leeni were talking quietly, but both jerked their heads toward him in surprise.

"What is it?" Leeni asked while Yoder jumped off the rock he'd sat upon and started toward The Wizard.

"What's wrong?" the boy asked.

The Wizard cleared his throat, regaining his composure a bit. "I've found it, I think. Deeper into the mountain, there's an expanse. A ledge winds upward to an exit in the back of the mountain's peak. I tried to reach it, but there's something in that cavern." He looked at Yoder with great confusion and some tangible fear. "It saw me, whatever it was. It saw my magic and dispelled it."

Yoder didn't understand. "What do you mean?" he asked, tilting his head. The Wizard explained.

"I cast a projection spell, sending my mind out into the tunnels to search for any anomalies that might be whatever destiny you are to fulfill. I found a cavern, but whatever lay within the cavern sensed my projected self and destroyed it. It felt like dying for a moment, or rather... like dying in a dream." The Wizard frowned, smoothing out his shirt to help regain some semblance of normalcy. Yoder looked, well, terrified.

Chapter Sixteen:
This doesn't feel right

Despite the fear The Wizard's words instilled, the troupe continued on The Wizard's path through the caverns. Their footfalls, Sixer's thumping, echoed loudly off the cavern walls and kept much of the dangers of the under-mountain away. Animals knew how to survive, avoiding larger predators, and all that noise certainly sounded like larger predators. This left the lot of them to their own thoughts, quietly navigating through rock spires across the cavern and tunnel floors.

The Wizard was most distressed of them all, pensive and almost paranoid. Every sound that echoed wrong made him turn to look, sometimes lifting his cane defensively. Yoder frowned, watching the man. It was even harder for him, who drew strength from The Wizard's faith. The boy moved closer to his guide and companion.

"Hey," he called out gently, flinching when The Wizard aimed his cane at him. "It's just me," Yoder announced with a raised hand.

The Wizard glared at him. "I'm fine." he said firmly.

"You're not," Yoder replied just as firmly. "You're scared. I'm always scared, so I get it." The Wizard harrumphed, refusing to commit to anything stubbornly. Yoder simply continued talking. "If you're scared, then I'm going to be more scared because you're scared, and you don't get scared. I don't know if I can be brave if you're scared," he admitted, which softened The Wizard's demeanor.

The older man switched his cane to his right hand, lifting the left to brush through his shaggy brown locks. "Fair enough. I shall try not to appear too perturbed, but we go carefully, please. If my magics are useless to us in the coming conflict, I cannot help you beyond whacking whatever it is with my cane."

Yoder grinned. "My best work so far's been poking things with my sword over my shield, so I'm glad for your whacking skills if it's a fight we're in for." Yoder's brows furrowed for a moment, his gaze lowering thoughtfully, then lifting up to The Wizard again. "We've faced everything else so far. What's one more to see the world saved?"

The Wizard chuckled, nodding. "Aye. One more conflict. If we're lucky." He added with a smile.

"Maybe you'll finally tell us who you are," Yoder suggested playfully, moving off to catch up with Leeni and Sixer.

"I've already told you repeatedly, boy. I'm The Wizard," the older man replied, twirling his cane in a manner more befitting his natural state.

Yoder rolled his eyes. "We know that. The Wizard of What?" he asked, walking right into it yet again.

"Yes." The Wizard replied immediately, grinning from ear to ear. Yoder didn't fall fully for it, though.

"The Wizard of Yes?" he asked, now grinning as well.

Leeni giggled, joining in. "Ohhh, that makes sense. Because he says Yes to things he shouldn't, like dangerous quests to save the world with a fat kid, a beautiful adventuress, a small dragon, and a…." She trailed off, looking at the lumbering giant that was Sixer and finding herself at a loss for words to describe him. "…. metal man?"

Sixer's head sphere swiveled toward Leeni, blue lights expanding as wide as they could. "Thank you, comrade," he said tinnily.

The Wizard huffed. "Could be. If you must know, it's an affectation that I earned in my youth. Sort of…. taking a joke and making it a legend. All the Mirrored Circle now refers to me as such because I am the most capable."

Yoder looked at Leeni, who chose to take point. "Uh huh. So, you're the most powerful mage in the whole Mirrored Circle?" Leeni asked incredulously, giving The Wizard a most unconvinced look. "And that's why you're here in the Razor's Teeth with us, cause this quest required the most powerful mage."

The Wizard scoffed. "If you two brats had any clue, you'd be biting your tongues right now. Politics and power often go hand in hand, but are not mutually exclusive," he explained. "All magic relies upon faith. Faith that something so…unseen, so enigmatic can exist. A man may wave his hands and recite a cantrip, but without faith in God and magic? It means nothing. Only the truest believers who've practiced the incantations, devoted their lives to the science of magic, have the faith necessary to touch the ethereal and change the energy of the world into a spell to be cast."

Yoder found it all very fascinating, but in a manner like a mundane person found quantum physics. Confusing but interesting. "So, if I learned these cantrips from you and I have faith in God and magic then I could cast spells?" he asked curiously. Leeni seemed to want to know too, nodding to Yoder's question.

The Wizard chuckled. "Aye, possibly, but time and experience dictate the power of the spells you learn. Just like wielding a sword, it takes practice to accomplish yourself," he said, his words echoing off the cavern walls after Yoder's own.

"That would help a lot, being able to use magic and swords? Think about all the adventures we could have with magic to protect and aid us," mentioned Leeni, full of fanciful dreams. "We could cut through armies with that kind of power," she added, to which the Wizard replied gravely.

"And that is why we do not accept just anyone into the Circle, magic can upset the balance of the world if used improperly. That is what gives us Garrick Thains."

Yoder grew tense at the name, the most notorious evil in Halziyon. He'd heard incredible stories about the brutality and callousness of the Black Vanguard, Thain's army. It stood to reason that if the soldiers were such terrible people, their leader must be impossibly worse. He feared ever meeting the overlord of Kurn.

The Wizard smiled, patting Yoder on the shoulder. "So, we take great care, as best we can, to eliminate any chances of the darker minded learning such power regardless of their faith but we are only men. God is infallible, we are not."

Sixer's head-sphere spun around, owlishly looking back at the others with his two blue lights. "I am detecting an intense energy ahead," he resonated tinnily, drawing everyone's attention except Perrixstar who was curled up on Yoder's head to nap because his shoulder was too small to lay upon.

The Wizard frowned. "That must be what disrupted my projection spell, it means we're close to the chasm chamber. Be on your guard, all of you," he advised, prompting Yoder and Leeni to draw their weapons.

Yoder secured his shield on his arm, gripping the hand-strap firmly in his gloved hand. "Okay, everyone. Let's go slow from here on."

Sixer remained ahead, thumping through the cavernous tunnels loudly while Yoder, Leeni, and The Wizard followed in that order. Yoder kept his shield in front of him, the wolf's head looking out from the center of the sturdy wooden circle braced with steel. Leeni moved behind him, the curved, razor-sharp dirk held underhanded in her left for her sword arm was splinted. The Wizard followed behind, his cane swung up and set on his shoulder rather than clacking away on the stone floor with every set of steps.

Passing from the huge tunnel to the even more massive chamber gave all but Sixer pause. The machine's foot-weights barely fit on the winding stone ledge that spiraled up the circumference of the chasm when the group began to ascend, causing them to stop and reorder themselves with Yoder at the forward position and Sixer behind them all. No matter how quietly each tried to step, the sound echoed everywhere in the dark expanse. Stealth was not an option.

Yoder grew tired after what felt like a full bell's time of walking round and around, upward and onward along the never-ending ledge. He glanced over the side, looking down and felt a brief wave of nausea hit him as the expanse opened up into darkness so thick that it seemed bottomless below. "This doesn't feel right." Yoder mumbled, leaning toward the assurance of the rough-hewn wall more until the desire to evacuate his bowels subsided. He swallowed hoarsely what felt like a mouth full of sand and paused, looking back to ask for the waterskin.

The group stopped there, taking a rest to drink water from the skin as it was passed about. Even Perrixstar took part, licking from the fount as Yoder poured some on his head to cool his rattled nerves. The liquid helped; a comforting chill temperature staved off the sweat that had been beading his dirty forehead. He passed the water skin back to The Wizard through Leeni and then readied his sword and shield once more. "Okay," the young man said, feeling more sure of himself as he began to march up the angled ledge again.

"The energy signature is growing stronger, we are approaching its location," Sixer announced, his already echoed voice resounding off the walls. Below, a faint keening sound was heard as some beast in the depths reacted to the noise. Yoder, Leeni, and The Wizard all looked up, squinting into the darkness but it was The Wizard who saw it first.

"There!" He called out, stretching an arm over their heads to point up into the distance. Yoder and Leeni both strained to see, noting a small mote of what appeared to be light. No larger than a star in the sky outside at night, but it was there all the same. "That's what I saw. When I drew close to it, something attacked my projection," The Wizard explained, excitement in his tone. "Our objective is there, I'm sure of it."

With their destination in sight, but far away; Yoder picked up the pace and the others followed. Ascending the ledge toward a tangible goal was far easier than walking without end had been, Yoder realized as he found renewed strength in his boot falls. He felt the same excitement that The Wizard displayed surging through his legs and arms, the thrill of the journey's end. They still had far to go, but the light at the end of the tunnel called to him in a way the boy had never felt before. Something…. special was waiting on the other side of that light.

Yoder stepped on something soft, it screeched madly and made him scream in that terribly uncourageous keen of his as he jerked his boot off of whatever it was and stumbled back into Leeni. Leeni caught him, but being smaller, was shoved back into The Wizard who toppled like the last domino with a mighty thump against Sixer's metal torso. "Oof!" The Wizard exclaimed. "What the hell was that?" he called out, trying to get Leeni back on her footing with a push.

The darkness erupted in keening cries and a cacophony of flapping sounds as bats swarmed off the rocks and out of a small crevasse in the wall. Yoder tried to get his balance, pulling his shield up in front of his face as he felt them battering at its surface. Leeni screamed in fright behind him, her dirk clattering on the stone ledge as she frantically swatted her hand about her head.

"It's in my hair!" she shrilly cried out. It was Sixer who saved the day, supporting The Wizard without concern while emitting a low, loud hum of processing power from his metal core. The hum began to rise in volume but not pitch, and the fluttering frenzy of bats were highly offended by the sound.

The swarm banked, swooping away from the disruptive noise out into the open expanse of the chasm, where they funneled upward in a chaotic tornado of winged motion. Yoder got his feet flat on the stone, stepped forward to give Leeni room, and kept his shield raised high just in case. Leeni recovered, crouching down to grab her blade then stepped up behind Yoder despite being wary of the wall now just as much as the bottomless pit over the ledge.

The Wizard just laughed it off. "Bats, nothing more. Everyone alright?"

Each member of the party checked in with an affirming nod or word. Yoder lowered his shield and walked with more care once again onward up the ledge, Leeni behind him and so on. Each of them was now more aware of their surroundings, more concerned with threats in the dark where the small lights of the ensorcelled equipment and Sixer's gaze did not illuminate.

Higher and higher, they ascended and the more they circled the chasm along that ledge; the larger the light above became. Yoder reasoned that it was an exit of some kind, a cavern mouth leading outside where the natural light of the day must be reaching in. After all this time in the dark, he longed for the bright sunshine again. So much so that he could almost imagine the warmth on his cheeks, it made him smile.

Sixer hummed, his two blue lights snapped upward. "Warning, elevated energy levels detected." The three looked up as well, seeing for just a moment that there was a bright white light growing in the center of the expanse above them. It looked to be mere feet from the opening they strove to reach high at the top of the massive chasm.

The Wizard's fearful voice called out. "Watch out!" As a frightening, deafening noise echoed off the chasm walls all around them. Yoder ran forward, turning to put his back against the wall with his shield raised just as the white light blinded them all and each was startled by the sound of a thunderclap.

When the light faded and their eyesight returned, Yoder and Leeni both gasped at the empty space Yoder had been standing. There, upon the rock face was a scorched mark of red stones, superheated by something so hot that they looked like coals in a stove.

"Oh, my God!" Yoder exclaimed in fear. "Run!" And run, he did. Surging from the wall, rushing up the ledge ahead of the group. Leeni called his name, but he didn't stop. She chased after him, The Wizard in toe behind her.

"Wait! I... oh blast it!" the foppish man called out, waving a hand to dismiss the light from his cane's crystal tip.

Another pulse of light burst from the ceiling, blindingly blasting at the rock wall behind Yoder's panicked form. It left hot rock smoldering in its wake and made the boy run even harder. Leeni skid to a stop when the blast went off, recovering her vision to give chase after her friend again.

The Wizard glanced back at Sixer. "Optical lights off, switch to night mode only." He demanded, the machine humming in response before the two blue lights winked out in his head-sphere. Satisfied, The Wizard turned forward and started to race after the teens.

"Yoder! It's targeting magic! Your shield, boy! Show me your shield!" The Wizard called out, trying to catch up to Leeni while Sixer continued at a slower pace due to his movement mechanisms. He had no way to run, for he was designed never to need to. Yoder heard The Wizard, watching above for the next shot and when it came flashing down at him; he turned back and returned to Leeni who was between them. The Wizard caught up, waving his hand at Yoder's shield to break the light enchantment. It winked out, the three stood still and waited.

Minutes passed without an attack. Yoder and Leeni looked to The Wizard for confirmation, who stared up at the empty blackness with a worried expression. "That...seems to have done the trick. So, no spells from here on out, it seems," he said, sighing. The Wizard hated feeling useless.

Yoder saw the sad expression. "Don't worry, we'll take care of it. Maybe this is why you needed me, no mage could fight this thing off," he suggested, nodding to Leeni before starting upward again along the ledge.

Leeni smiled at The Wizard, nodding as well. "We got this." She encouraged him, trying to cheer the man up before she moved to follow Yoder with her weapon in hand. He followed them, still frustrated with the impotence of not being able to use his spells to help these two. An unlikely hero and a small girl dreaming of greater things. Somehow, the thought of the two did bring him hope and he closed his eyes for a moment to silently say a prayer.

His devotion was interrupted by Leeni's cry, brown eyes flicking open just in time to be blinded by a flash of light from above. Yoder dodged it, but barely and was trying to pick himself back up off the ground with sword and shield in hand. Leeni rushed to help him, throwing her dirk down.

"What happened? Why is it attacking?" he asked of the darkness. "There's no more magic!" He called out, confused and frustrated. As Leeni helped Yoder to his feet, the bright light rose above again. The Wizard watched in horror as it grew in brilliance, and the teens were not ready for it.

He looked to see Leeni gather her weapons, Yoder watching her and thanking her for her help. Both were oblivious to the blast that would come in a moment. "Yoder!!" The Wizard bellowed, rushing forward as fast as he could, but he knew he was too far away. The boy had to move, somehow. His mind raced, trying to think of a way to save him. There was only one. "Invocatio Spiritus!" The Wizard called out, thrusting a hand forward to enact the simplest of spells in his repertoire. All it would do was reveal magic to him, but he hoped the casting would draw the deadly attack to him instead.

The last thing The Wizard saw…. was a flash of bright, white light. Heat overwhelmed him, he heard screaming ahead of him and closed his eyes. *Them or me, make it be me.* He thought peacefully. *O Lord God. Hallowed be thy name. Thy Kingdom Come. Thy Will Be Done on Earth as it is in Heaven…*

CHAPTER SEVENTEEN:
Don't give up

An anguished cry brought The Wizard's eyes opened, blinking in the dark after such bright light blinded him. He was not dead, a fact that surprised him greatly. He looked down at himself but saw with horror that at his feet lay the smoldering, prone body of the small, faerie dragon. Perrixstar mewled, burnt and blackened flesh and sinew where once beautiful, shimmering scales were now smoked and charred. One of the dragon's wings was obliterated, reduced to nothing but ash while the other twitched against the dark, unforgiving stone.

"Oh god...," The Wizard whispered, sinking to his knees.

Yoder crashed to the ground near him on the ledge, his jowled cheeks tight and red. "Perri!" The boy whimpered, tears streaming down his scrunched and ugly expression. Leeni stood over the boy with restrained, but white-knuckled rage as Yoder unclasped his cloak and tried to carefully bundle the dying dragon in it. "Don't worry, we'll fix you up somehow. Somehow," the boy stammered, his voice cracking with the tension of sorrow in his throat.

The Wizard's sharp featured face turned cold; his brown eyes full of anger. "Give me the dragon, lad. I will draw the blasts while the rest of you ascend and destroy whatever it is above us," he said firmly, lifting his cane and touching the bottom tip with his fingertips. "Confige." He said to it, then drove the tip into the stone like it was sand to leave the cane standing upright. "Go!" He said earnestly, taking the bundled beast into his arms and cuddling it close to his chest with one limb cradled under the bulk.

Yoder couldn't find words, but a surge of fury replaced his sadness at the fallen creature and its sacrifice. He turned, pushing around Leeni and ran up the ledge with a hard grip on his sword and shield-strap. Leeni followed behind him, her pretty face a mask of emptiness belying the storm inside her. Not only was she angry over the injury of her friend, a mythical creature of beauty; but she raged over the tears of Yoder ahead of her. For once, he cried not for himself and Leeni Vex found that she hated the sight and sound more than anything in the world.

The Wizard slipped past Sixer, moving back down the ledge a ways while the white light above began to illuminate and signal a new attack. Sixer stomped forward, slower but following the two angry teens. He felt nothing for the dragon, he was a machine and did not have feelings. However, his devotion to Yoder and the goal of his new communion dictated that he aid them and so the construct marched on.

With the mewling dragon firmly held in his arm, wrapped like a babe in swaddle; The Wizard thrust his free, right hand toward his cane. "Protego!" He called to it, the cane's crystal tip flashing brilliant bluish energy. When the blast rained down at the cane, a barrier erupted from the crystal tip to deflect it. A shower of sparks exploded around the barrier of energy, but to The Wizard's dismay, the spell was broken by the blast. He frowned, swiping his fingers this way and that way quickly while the light above charged up again. "Ditans guttura voluntatem…. protego!"

Once again, the crystal tip of his cane embedded in the rock ledge flashed blue energy and the second blast that lanced through the dark at the cane was met with another barrier which caught the attack but was summarily dispelled. "Damn it." The Wizard muttered to himself, unable to sustain the defense of his cane. He had no choice but to keep whatever it was above him occupied with constant recasting for as long as his will would hold. He hoped Yoder and the others would stop it in time.

Charging up the ledge and circling the empty chasm, Yoder found his courage in the anger over Perrixstar. His blood drummed in his ears and a feeling rose up from deep in his gut that he didn't quite understand but needed to be released. It came in the form of a grunting growl as he found renewed vigor. The higher he ran, the brighter the light from that hole above became and the illumination helped him see his target. It looked like a giant worm hanging from the ceiling of the chasm, one long tendril glowing a faint blue between what appeared to be large, white scales.

Yoder could hardly grasp the sight of the thing. At its end was a huge, glowing eyeball that stared down from on high in a magnificently terrifying manner. It was that eye that fired the bolts of white light down at them all this time, he realized, after watching it launch two volleys of energy down at The Wizard below them.

Leeni called from behind Yoder. "How are we supposed to reach that thing?!" Which was a very good question. Yoder didn't know yet, frantically looking for some way to reach it from the ledge.

The eye began to charge another bolt, its pupil glowing brighter and brighter before Yoder and Leeni's very eyes. Sixer continued to march up the ledge but was well far behind and below at the moment, so he was of no use to the two. Yoder shoved his sword into its sheath, backing up against the wall before unstrapping his shield and setting it beside him.

"If I die.... take care of Perri for me," he said to the girl as she came to stop near him, looking back and forth between the boy and the monstrous white worm.

"...What? What are you doing?"

"Being the hero," Yoder said, grinning over at Leeni despite the strong desire to piss himself. He was less afraid of the worm than the fall down to wherever the end of the chasm was.

Leeni grabbed him by his chain-covered shoulder with her dirk hand. "No way. You can't!"

The blonde boy looked over at her, fearful but resolved. "I have to. For Perrixstar, for The Wizard." He pulled his shoulder from her grasp, nodding. "Look at it this way, you might be rid of me now!" He tried to joke, scooting out of her reach and inhaling a deep breath.

"Idiot! I..." Leeni started to respond, but closed her mouth and watched the insane boy looking over the white worm.

Yoder eyed it intently, shaking out his free hands before he charged toward the ledge. It was only a few steps, but he couldn't afford to miss. The last step, he pushed off as hard as he could and threw his arms up as far as they'd reach. The ground gave way to darkness under him, and Yoder thought this was the end until his bulk smacked into the white worms' scaley side, and he scrambled to grab hold of the edge of one of those scales. Leeni screamed, almost stabbing herself in the face with her own dirk as she drew it up to her mouth instinctively when the boy jumped.

The Wizard was already sweating, droplets ran down his face as he recast the defensive spell over and over again upon the cane to keep those terrible white blasts of energy busy. Unaware of all that happened above them, the only thing he could hear was the echo of a scream and it made his blood run cold. However, the white light was growing up above and he had to be ready for the next volley, so he pushed himself to cast again. He could only believe in the three above him, for he could not see them.

Yoder clung to the white worm's scale that he'd caught a hand on, the other slipped off and now hung down at his side while he dangled over the chasm. Terror gripped his heart. "Ohhhhhhhhh my Goooooooood. This was a bad idea!" he cried out.

Leeni groaned. "Of course, it was! Now what?!" She called from the ledge, unable to reach, and left to witness Yoder's idiotic attempt at suicide.

While Sixer continued to march, growing closer and closer to the turn where Leeni stood ahead; the machine watched Yoder's dangling, plump shape hanging off the side of the white worm's long, round form. Yoder fumbled to draw his sword. "I'm going to try to stab between the scales, maybe I can kill it!" He bellowed, kicking his fat feet in their worn boots idly below him.

"It's going to kill you, stupid!" Leeni bellowed back as the white light from its eye grew brighter and brighter.

A crackling burst of energy erupted from the eye of the worm, causing its body to jerk backward with the force of its expelling. Yoder screeched, losing his grip on the sword in its sheath. Luckily it sank back down rather than falling out, but the boy was more concerned with holding on tight to the scale. "No!" he moaned wretchedly, hanging tight until the worm relaxed and stopped moving again. His free hand fumbled at his sword once more.

Leeni didn't want to leave the ledge, watching in horror as Yoder struggled with life and death dangling from the side of the massive worm. She saw him reach for his sword again, inhaling sharply as he drew the blade free and tried to aim the tip between the scales in front of him. Aiming the blade seemed fruitless though, Yoder's arm was too shaky to hold it steady. A stroke of inspiration overtook him then, remembering how he wielded his sword with his shield. The boy changed methods, putting the tip against the edge of one scale to use the hard surface like his shield and steady the blade.

His arms were exhausted, one arm holding all his girth while the other gave as mighty a heave as his pudgy body could give. The sword sunk into the worm just above the scales around the eye stalk, but no blood gushed from the wound like it had when he stabbed that guard or all those gnolls. Sparks of lightning shot out of the space between, singing Yoder and the boy twitched at the sudden lancing pain. His grip on the sword handle tightened reflexively, even as his other hand let go of the scale. His fingers felt numb, his heart jumped into his throat as he swung down to hang off the sword hilt instead.

Leeni screamed again, throwing down her weapon behind her before thrusting her hand out uselessly. She'd never reach him, but by

God, she wanted to. "Yoder! Don't let go!" Yoder desperately tried to get his other hand around the sword's hilt to hold on, feet kicking wildly under him. "Don't give up! Just hold on!" she cried, losing her resolve as tears began to well in her eyes. She watched, full of fear and doubt from the ledge as Yoder fought to survive.

The eye of the white worm had gone dark when the sword pierced through it, cutting wiring and cords that channeled energy through to the optical cannon. Sparks shot from its base; circuitry damaged. The white worm began to process repair mode, sending tiny machines through its internal structure toward the invasive sword to patch the cords and wires that made up its inner circuitry but even as it did so; Yoder's weight made the sword wrench upward and cut the main power line running through its center. The worm twitched once then fell inert. The spikes of its tail that kept it moored into the rock ceiling retracted and with a great rumbling, the worm began to slide from its burrow with Yoder still hanging from it.

Yoder cried out in surprise as the worm began to fall from the ceiling. "Leeni! Help!" Was all he could get out before the tail end of the great worm slipped free and Yoder felt the nightmarish rush of air as he and it began to tumble downward. He closed his eyes tight, waiting for death with no escape in sight. Leeni dropped down to her knees on the ledge, almost falling over it herself with how far she leaned as she watched the monster and the boy drop toward the dark.

Sixer saw the fall coming, turning toward the chasm. His internal processing unit hummed loudly, calculating acceleration, distance, vectors, lengths and diameters in mere moments. His two blue lights flicked on in his head sphere and the construct ballooned suddenly as its center plates extended outward. He picked up a footplate and hurled it like a discus out into the chasm at the falling worm, past its eye. The body hit the foot-weight's tube and the weight came swinging back around again like a lasso. It spun, twisting around the worm's head and Yoder too.

A moment after the foot-weight released, Sixer swung his arms backward and jammed his massive metal fingers into the rock wall behind him. His fingers locked in at an angle after piercing stone, mooring them to the wall so when the force of the worm's fall pulled on his body; the internal cranks loudly whined trying to compensate. Sixer was pulled over the ledge as the worm went down, holding tight to the wall and suspended there.

Further below, The Wizard cuddled Perrixstar bundled in the blanket and watched for another volley burst but none came. Instead, his horrified eyes turned wide as the massive, white-scaled worm came tumbling down toward him. "Bloody Hell!" he cried out, turning away to shield the injured dragon with his body as the worm was lassoed by Sixer's leg tube and swung with a crash into the rock wall. As the dust and debris settled, The Wizard heard a soft groan. "Good heavens," he mumbled, crawling over the wrecked worm carefully.

He found Yoder, half-conscious and covered in rock dust. The boy was flopped over the worm's bulk, pinned to it by Sixer's leg tube. "Yoder! C'mon, lad. Speak to me!" The Wizard cried out, scrambling to reach him. Yoder groaned again, almost in reply. The Wizard gently set Perrixstar down, climbing up onto the worm's length to work the boy free of Sixer's tube and drag him down to the ledge. The worm shifted, scraping against the ledge and the stone started to crack. "Up, boy. Up! We have to go! Here!" Hoping Perrixstar's body would ignite something in Yoder, The Wizard lifted the swaddle and pushed it gingerly to Yoder's chest.

Yoder was barely aware, heavy dead weight sinking as The Wizard pulled him down off the worm but as soon as he felt the cloth of his cloak against him; the boy curled his weary arms around it protectively. "Per... ri," he mumbled, dizzy and disoriented.

"Aye, lad. We must get Perrixstar to safety. Quickly, with me." The Wizard said, patting Yoder on the shoulder and starting to climb over the worm's body while it was still suspended by Sixer's grasp.

Yoder followed, almost on autopilot and guided only by the desire to save his little friend. Perrixstar mewled hoarsely between the folds of the wrapped cloak and that sound brought Yoder more awareness.

He blinked, leaving a trail of stone dust behind him as he fumbled and stumbled over the worm after The Wizard toward where the cane was still embedded in the ledge. The barrier spell had protected it from the worm's crash and The Wizard grasped onto it to pull himself fully free of the coiled, dead worm. He turned back, holding a hand out to Yoder to help him traverse to safety next.

Leeni ran as fast as she could back down the spiraling ledge, crying and sniffling till she reached the ball-shaped Sixer blocking her path and extended down into the chasm. "What.... what are you doing??" she called out, coming to stop to catch her breath.

Sixer's head sphere rotated, blue lights aiming at the girl. "I have caught the creature and secured it so The Wizard may rescue Yoder, Comrade. My optical sensors indicate that this has been a successful act and our companions are now safe. I will begin extricating myself from the creature now," he said tinnily, the cranking mechanisms inside his bulk retracting the foot weight and tube slowly but steadily. Leeni let out a strangled gasp, devolving into sobs as she tipped and slid down the wall.

As The Wizard took up his cane with one hand and put his other around Yoder to help him walk, the two struggled up the ledge carefully before Sixer untangled and the great white worm slid off the ledge to tumble all the way down the chasm. Yoder couldn't tell how long it took before he heard the crash and really didn't care anymore. His friends were safe. The boy cuddled Perrixstar in his cloak and pushed onward, numb with shock and confusion.

By the time the two reached Sixer's rounded form still bound to the ledge, he had retracted his leg and foot weight fully. His two blue lights fixed on The Wizard and Yoder when they were in view, tracking their progress. "Leeni Vex, our compatriots are near," he announced to the girl in a resonant tone. Leeni lifted her head, face red from sobbing and she began to wipe her features clean in an effort to compose herself before they arrived.

Sixer began the process of condensing his plating again, shifting each one outward and inward along each other until he had slimmed back down. Lastly, the construct straightened his fingers and pulled his massive hands from the stone so they could hang loosely at his sides. Both Leeni and the machine watched The Wizard hold Yoder up while they approached.

The Wizard looked up with a worn smile. "All is well. Leeni, come take Perrixstar from Yoder. Thank you."

The girl all but ran to Yoder's other side, gently taking the bundled dragon from her injured friend. Yoder was wheezing but stayed on his feet all the same. "...th-thanks," he mumbled, still in shock.

The Wizard produced his water skin, putting it in the boy's hands. "Drink, my boy. Drink and rest," he said softly, guiding Yoder to lean on the wall while he drank the cool water slowly.

Chapter Eighteen:
Is that what I think it is?

Yoder took only minutes to rest, drinking his fill from the water skin. "How's Perrixstar?" he asked, no longer feeling hoarse and dizzy.

Leeni shook her head sadly, holding the bundled beast to her chest. "It's barely moving. I don't know what to do," she said, sniffling. Yoder looked to The Wizard with a plea in his sorrowful, blue eyes.

"Can you do something?" he asked, like a small child confronted with death for the first time.

The Wizard smiled, shaking his head. "I can ease the pain, but I cannot heal its body. I'm sorry, lad."

While the three were recovering, Sixer had strode onward to scout and secure the area. His sensors reached far and wide but found nothing to disrupt their rest until he looked out through the exit in the rock wall. Blue lights widened as big as they could. "I am able to assist Perrixstar," he resonated tinnily, turning his metal body around fully so he might look upon his companions. Yoder and Leeni both looked to the construct in awed surprise, neither expecting Sixer to be capable.

The Wizard squinted, incredulous. "How?" he asked.

"We will take Perrixstar to the medical center," Sixer stated.

"What medical center? What are you talking about?" The Wizard replied curiously, brows furrowing.

"We have arrived," Sixer said cryptically.

"Arrived where?" Yoder asked, pushing off the wall to walk toward the machine. Sixer turned sideways and stepped back, giving Yoder full view of what lay beyond the brightened portal. "Oh my god…" Yoder said. "Is that what I think it is?"

Leeni's curiosity piqued, the girl slipped up beside Yoder to look out with him before she let out a surprised gasp. The Wizard followed, brows rising on his sharply featured face. There, beyond the arch of the rocky opening, sprawled a most majestic and massive cityscape of gleaming metals. Spires with round, pointed tips like dollops of cream on a cake reached toward the bright, blue sky. Sunshine brightened every surface to a glistening radiance Yoder had never seen before.

He was drawn to it, stepping forward through the opening out onto the rocky ledge beyond. He looked down, finding the mountain's back face stretching down beyond his range of vision and the height made him dizzy. Leeni had cradled her dirk to hold the bundled dragon with her splinted limb, reaching out to grasp Yoder's arm with the other hand when she joined him. The two looked back to the gleaming city before them, with high, smooth walls of silver dotted in perfect symmetry by capped towers.

In the distance, between the high spires, beautifully constructed buildings with swooping arches and open balconies shone brightly. No plants or banners hung from or decorated any of the buildings. For all the two could see, this magical city was empty. No man stood watch in any of the wall towers, and no people moved upon the balconies or in the windows of the spires and houses.

Black roads crisscrossed between the tall buildings and towers, separating them like streams of ink on a map and tall, thin wooden poles protruded up alongside the roads where strange ropes ran from one to the next onward, and onward. Some diverted at intersecting roads, creating an odd, but simple grid pattern that somehow made the city easier to understand by scale. If both were not witnessing the view together, either one might believe it to be an illusion, a mirage of some sort. Nothing so beautiful and alien could exist that was more grand and glorious than the city before them.

The Wizard stepped through next, followed by Sixer who had to bend down to make it out into the sunlight. He stopped behind the two, peering over their heads with a look of utter awe that he rarely ever showed the world. "I do believe…. we have found the lost kingdom of Solaria…," he announced in a hushed whisper, truly beside himself at the gift God had granted him for his faith. "Bastion of culture, of magic and science. The last great kingdom of history."

Yoder felt inspired to say something, listening to The Wizard's speech but he could find no greater words to say than one. It tumbled out of his slack jaw thoughtlessly, but it echoed in the hearts of both Leeni and The Wizard. "…. Wow…."

Sixer hummed. "I am registering no power nor life signs. The city is dead," he announced tinnily. Those words snapped the three back to reality and each of them looked away from the wondrous view to stare at the construct.

"What do you mean dead?" asked Yoder.

"The city of Solaria is powered by energy coalesced into crystalline structures; these structures are implanted into generators that divert trace energy through conduits throughout the city's infrastructure. Without crystals, the city's power systems and defenses are inert. The city is dead." Sixer resonated from his compact chest chamber.

Leeni drew in a sharp breath, asking, "But wait, does that mean your medical center won't be able to save Perrixstar?"

"That is correct, unless we replace the empty crystals with fresh energized crystalline forms; we will not be able to power the city and the medical center," Sixer explained.

Yoder frowned, shaking his head firmly. "No, we're going in there and we're going to save Perrixstar. You're a worker, Sixer. How do we locate and install new crystals?"

Sixer hummed. "It is possible there are stores of crystals in the power department warehouse. The likelihood of energized crystals is low as they have been in storage for two hundred years."

Yoder looked confused. "Years?" he asked curiously. Sixer replied. "A year is a measure of Solarian time, recognized as the passage of four separate seasons."

Yoder nodded. "A seasonal cycle. Got it." His brows remained furrowed, pensively considering their next move.

The Wizard smiled, watching. "Perhaps Sixer might locate harvestable crystals?" he advised gently, prompting the boy to look at his friend, the machine.

Sixer hummed. "I am capable of doing so," he resonated.

"We're going to need to rest, the three of us. We'll make our way down and enter the city, find somewhere to settle in. I need you to make Perrixstar comfortable," Yoder said to The Wizard, who gave a nod in return and moved closer to Leeni. "Leeni, we'll take shifts watching over Perri so each of us can get some sleep and explore the city. My priority is saving Perri's life." Leeni nodded as well, showing the bundle to The Wizard who hovered his cane over the injured dragon and began to chant softly.

Yoder turned to Sixer next. "Your mission is to find an energized crystal and get the city's power back on, at least enough to make this medical center of yours work. Once Perrixstar's safe, we'll worry about defenses and…," He was cut off as Sixer's blue lights widened.

"Warning. Proximity alert," the construct said, turning away to face the opening back into the chasm.

Yoder grimaced, reaching for his sword. "Where?" he asked, stepping defensively in front of Leeni's back to cover her and The Wizard while they tended to the Faerie Dragon.

"Below, at the bottom of the chasm," Sixer stated.

Yoder moved around him, returning through the opening to peer down into the dark. Tiny lights moved in the blackness; Yoder assumed they were torches. "Damn," he muttered to himself, backing away and sheathing his sword. "It has to be the Black Vanguard. They followed us. We should move, make for the city now," he said as he exited the cavern once more, looking for a way down. "Here," he beckoned to the others, finding a path down the mountain's face.

The Wizard finished chanting, bathing the small dragon in soft, golden light. Leeni huddled the bundle closer to her chest and moved to follow Yoder once The Wizard gave her a nod to go. He followed close behind. "The spell should keep it asleep for a few hours without pain," he said softly, saddened by Perrixstar's state after such a sacrifice. To be in agony after saving him from certain doom, The Wizard felt responsible and more than a little guilty. It showed on his worried face.

Yoder felt the pain in his gut, his mind worried over the small dragon's fate as he started down the rough path. It was hard to enjoy the excitement of the city ahead when his thoughts agonized over Perrixstar. Leeni walked behind him, holding the bundle in both her arms now to keep the creature steady and safe. She too was preoccupied with Perrixstar's health and safety, but resolutely marched on.

Two bells of silent, grueling travel down the mountain passed. As the group approached the open gates of Solaria City, Yoder marveled at the massive archway situated only tens of steps from the mountain's face between. "This doesn't make sense. Why is the city here? There's no road, no way out of the mountains that I can see," he remarked, looking around him.

The Wizard followed Leeni past the boy, shrugging his shoulders. "The makers, as Sixer calls them, were known for magic. Perhaps they had other means of transportation that did not require roads."

"Incorrect. While other methods of travel were available, this is not the original location of Solaria City. My processing unit cannot comprehend the purpose of its repositioning to this location, there is no logical reason for it. Yoder is correct, this makes no sense," Sixer replied tinnily.

The Wizard raised a brow, turning his attention upon the street that stretched beyond the archway into the city. It was made of what appeared to be obsidian stone, but as he stepped onto it his expression grew confused. "This is not stone, it feels…off." His booted foot stomped on the darkened surface.

"A mixture of carbon, hydrogen, and sulphur, a byproduct of the mining process that my manufactory line employed. The Makers found use for it as a malleable substance that bonds and hardens as it dries. It is called Asphalt," Sixer explained, standing on the road behind them all. "The Makers instructed assembly units to mold and shape roads with the mixture for ease of travel. A smooth, flat surface is more efficient to move upon than uneven earth." He resonated.

The Wizard looked quite fascinated, tapping on the asphalt road with the bottom of his cane curiously. "Marvelous. What are the buildings made of?"

"The city's structures are constructed with a silicate polymer over an aggregate cement blend called concrete. The silicate absorbs ambient sunlight which is converted into energy routed throughout the city to the power station for crystal infusion creating a renewable resource of unlimited power." Sixer continued to The Wizard's delight.

"Oh, that's brilliant! An entire city acting as a conduit for magical energy."

Sixer tinnily replied, "Incorrect. The power systems of the city are science, not magic."

The Wizard huffed. "You say po-tay-to, I say po-tah-to."

"We can learn about the city later," Yoder said, following The Wizard and waving for Leeni to come with him. "Let's go make camp in there." Motioning to the first of the small buildings that lined either side of the street. Each had the same, beautiful, sweeping arches and metal construction. Yoder guided Leeni into the circular doorway and the two looked around the room, finding a table and chairs and other strange pieces of furniture. All were covered in heavy, gray dust as if abandoned for a long time, showing signs of decay.

There were pots with no plants growing inside them and strange, glass windows mounted on the walls with no imagery behind them. Some of the cabinets reminded Yoder of his mother's kitchen but made of some smooth material that did not feel like metal while others were absolutely metal. When Yoder pulled open one of the larger metal cabinets, it was filled with desiccated things. Food possibly, now dried out and turning to dust like everything else. Worse still, it smelled horrible, and Yoder closed the door quickly before he felt the need to retch from the stink.

Leeni sat on the floor behind a large rectangular object that had once been orange. It was shaped like a chair, but stretched out and so provided good cover for the girl while she watched over the fallen Faerie Dragon. The girl was silent all this time, save for the occasional matronly cooing that she shared with the slumbering dragon wrapped in Yoder's cloak. There was little she could do for the once beautiful creature save give it peace and solace, which she dedicated herself to. Yoder watched her for a long while, fighting back the wretched sense of loss that soured his stomach more than the fetid stink in that cabinet he'd opened.

Yoder and The Wizard moved the table and chairs aside, and the empty pots and any other items were also shuffled closer to the walls so the two men could set up The Wizard's backup tent while Sixer kept watch outside. It did not take long for them to finish constructing it, nor did it take long to unroll the bedding and blankets inside.

"Here you go, Leeni," Yoder said softly, stepping out of the tent flaps. Leeni rose with a smile, carefully cradling her bundle before she walked across the floor and ducked into the tent to set up a blanket nest where Perrixstar could lay.

Yoder returned to the road, frowning as he looked around. "Sixer, go find your crystals. Get the power turned on," the boy said, scratching his jowly, round cheeks with one gloved hand while he considered his next step. The city's size was overwhelming, this one street alone held more buildings of varying size and luxury than he could search in a day.

Sixer hummed and began to stomp down the black road, accessing his internal schematics so he knew the exact streets to take to reach the power station. It was a massive, square structure in the heart of the city, but the sight of other worker constructs like himself in various states of disrepair strewn around the grounds of the power station did give the machine a moment's pause. They were not of his line, subtle variations in their exterior design were noted by Sixer and he reasoned that these were the next evolutionary step in his manufactory plan. Though Sixer could not feel emotions, there was a disquiet to see the younger, superior generation dead on the ground before him.

He continued, marching around the building to the worker's entrance which was made for something his size rather than a human's door. The bay gateway was locked, and his access codes were no longer functional, so the construct broke the lock with one of his wide, metal hands then drew the portcullis door upward. He walked inside on his two odd legs and his blue lights moved from side to side observing the complex interior of machines that once infused the city with power.

He found the power station generator, long shut down and covered in heavy dust like everything else. Sixer turned, opening crates that were once meant to store crystals but found the gems inside dull and empty of energy. He took one in hand, moving through the power station toward the Solarian rejuvenator machine. The large looming device was just as dead as the rest of the city. Sixer stared at it, humming softly as his core processed the conundrum of how to make power in order to re-energize a crystal. How to empower the power.

Back on the first street, The Wizard moved to stand at Yoder's side. "So, my boy. You've found a city thought to be lost to time itself, abandoned and empty. What will you do with it?" he asked curiously, smiling.

Yoder scowled. "I can't think about that now, we need to find a way to heal Perrixstar," he said.

The Wizard's smile soured, nodding. "And defend the city," he added, nudging Yoder with his right arm to get his attention. When the young man looked at him, The Wizard motioned upward toward the mountain.

There on the ledge where the entrance to the chasm was, small black shapes moved about. Yoder's face paled at first, then hardened in frustration. "Damn it," the boy cursed.

"It'll only be a matter of hours before they make it down the mountain, we'll have to hide or defend the city if we want any hope of healing the dragon," The Wizard said, watching the soldiers in the distance high above.

Yoder sighed. "Let's hope Sixer can find what he needs."

The Wizard nodded slowly. "So much for prophetic destiny, eh? You traveled all this way with a madman. I'm beginning to wonder if the prophecy was worth it. I'm sorry, lad," he admitted, apologizing for dragging him into this, for putting them all in danger.

Yoder put a hand on his sword hilt, shaking his head. "This is Solaria. There's something here that'll save the world and that's why we were guided to it. I'm just sorry you picked me by accident, I'll do my best though. For Perrixstar. For Leeni and Sixer and You."

The Wizard looked back at the overweight boy, once a sniveling, obnoxious child. "Best mistake I ever made," he said, like a proud father. Yoder blinked at him, those bright blue eyes beginning to shine with wetness. The Wizard rolled his eyes. "Oh, don't you start," he said, laughing lightly. "No time for tears, Yoder." The boy nodded, taking a deep breath to steady himself.

For an overweight, bumbling, bastard of a boy, Yoder Hals had given up the comfort of the familiar and the safety of home. He followed a dream, a choice made by a mysterious man who had coaxed the boy into experiencing the world around him for the first time. Now, he stood trapped within the walls of an ancient, once-lost city of immeasurable power and facing the greatest military threat that he knew of. With only his hopes and dreams to give him strength, Yoder looked to his companion with great pride.

Chapter Nineteen:
How impressive

In a cavern not far from the great chasm hours before, the bloody bodies of Gnolls who escaped the battle against the first invaders lay strewn across stone. Standing over the corpses, Atolicus Grehner and his regiment sheathed and secured their weapons. "Disgusting critters, gnolls." Atolicus spat, kicking the body of a small Gnoll who could not be more than a teen's age. His soldiers circled around him while he removed the finned black helm from his bald head.

"No sign of the intruders, Sir!" One barked to report, the rest standing at attention.

The captain rubbed his beard, cleaning flecks of Gnoll blood from it while considering his next move. The regiment had searched long and hard through these endless caverns and tunnels after coming upon the Gnoll forces slain in the tunnels, yet still did not find those who had broken into Kurn and eluded them since. His face contorted in anger. "Damn it all. Separate into pairs, one torch-bearer and one without spread through these tunnels and find the intruders! Now! I will contact our king and hope he does not order me to slaughter the lot of you! Cretins!"

The soldiers stiffened, paired up and fled their captain's wroth. Left alone, Atolicus tucked his helm under his arm and stalked back through the tunnels with haste. It took less than a bell's toll to reach the mouth of the caves and look upon the gray wastes of Kurn again now that he knew the way. Under the clouded sky, Atolicus retrieved the remnants of a black candle. He lit it with one of the torches left to mark the troop's passage then tossed the burning candle to the dirt. As the thick smoke billowed, it gathered into the miasmic cloud that allowed the captain to speak directly to Garrick Thain.

Thain's visage appeared in the smoke. "Report, Captain." The King of Kurn commanded. Atolicus cleared his throat.

"We have tracked the intruders to the Razor's Teeth, My King. Whoever they are, they fought half a nest of Gnolls and further penetrated the caverns within this mountain behind me. However, we lost the trail after that. My men are searching the tunnels as we speak and I am confident we will prevail," he said tersely, annoyed with the disruption and very much ready to kill these invaders then return to his squalidly life.

"I wish I shared your belief, Captain. Be that as it may, I am left with no choice but to lean upon your skills. Contact me the moment you have dispatched the interlopers, but I want the one with the cane alive. He and I have unfinished business," Thain said firmly.

Atolicus gave a curt nod. "As you desire, Your Majesty," he replied, while Garrick Thain dismissed the magical smoke with a wave of his hand. Atolicus watched the congealed cloud disperse and float apart on the faint breeze sweeping down from the mountain then turned to enter the caverns once more.

In his laboratory, Garrick Thain ran a manicured fingertip along his experimentation table's surface thoughtfully. He considered the impotence of his magic's range and potency ruefully. Even with the extra energy of the crystal matrix he wore in the rings on his hands, connected to the large edifice suspended on the observation deck; he could not penetrate the mountain range or see beyond it. This vexed the King of Kurn more and more with each passing day. How frustrating it was to rely on his peons with all his magical might. Idiots, the lot of them.

"Sir!" A soldier came clattering up the tunnel to meet Atolicus Grehner, pausing to salute. "We have located the remains of a monster in a massive chasm, freshly killed."

Atolicus nodded. "Show me," he replied, marching loudly through the tunnel while the soldier ran ahead to guide him. The captain considered this news gravely. If these intruders were powerful enough to slay a monstrous beast, then he must tread carefully. First, however, he must catch up to them.

The soldier guided him through the maze of caverns, a duo of his men joining them as he passed by each tunnel until the full complement was at his back once more. Atolicus felt bolstered by their presence as he always did, despite his abuse. Strength in numbers was the most effective and brutal means of settling disputes or defending oneself and while he had control of this squadron of the King's army, he was a powerful and safe man indeed.

As the regiment marched into the massive cavern where lay the ruined body of the white worm construct, the soldiers fanned out to block the entrance and better defend their leader as they had been taught. Atolicus Grehner regarded the great beast with a measured look at first that soon widened in awe. The creature was as long as a tree was tall, perhaps more and its white scales gleaned in the torchlight. He marveled at them then rolled his eyes upward to peer into the gloom above. No ceiling in sight.

"Sir, there is a ledge that appears to run along the walls of this cavern upward. Perhaps it leads to another cavern or tunnel above?" asked one of the soldiers, waving his torch to illuminate the ramp of the ledge from the floor.

Atolicus peered at it next, nodding in agreement. "We will investigate further. But first, I want this beast stripped down. Take its scales and whatever else useful we might find in its body. You," he pointed to a torchbearer soldier, motioning back out of the cavern. "Return to the Mines and fetch two carts, more men to carry this creature. Our king will want to examine it," he commanded, watching half his men descend upon the white worm and begin to pry off its plating. The other man exited the cavern, doing as he was told.

"You three, make camp. We're going to be here awhile," the captain grunted, motioning to three of his men who broke off from guarding the entrance and left to collect the supplies from outside on the cart they'd brought, now bearing one less horse as the runner had taken the other back to the Mines for reinforcements. Atolicus was brought the first scale of the white worm, which he hefted in his gauntleted hands and admired curiously. It was lighter than expected, but firm. Metal, not scale.

"Sir?" One of the soldiers breaking plating off the white worm called out, drawing Atolicus' attention. He set the plate in his hands down, stomping across the stone floor toward the soldier who pulled the plate he was breaking off open. "Look at this," he nodded to the innards of the beast. It had no blood, no bones. Atolicus took a torch from one of the others, sweeping it closer to the beast to inspect it. Within the white worm was only copper tubes, wires, and steel rods.

"...magic," Atolicus said, his expression souring. "Find a way to pull these rods and these copper things as well. Bring them to me when done."

Seating himself upon a rock, Atolicus knocked three times on the white worm's plating that he held in his hand. It felt sturdy and strong, but light of weight and easy to carry. The revelation and the stripping of the white worm's corpse had waylaid the Black Vanguard troop for the time being, but something didn't sit right with Atolicus Grehner while he watched and sometimes inspected the pieces of the creature that his men tore from its body and presented him. No blood. No organs or meat to cook and eat. He wondered what manner of beast only had metal inside of it.

Hours passed and when the forward scout returned to report that more men and two carts were on their way, the captain carried his new prize through the caverns now lit by torches to guide his way. He stepped out into the light of late day, the land already shadowed by the sun's lowering behind the smog's curtain. Again, he lit the candle and tossed it down to the dirt to await contact with his master.

When the cloud congealed into the shape of King Garrick's head, Atolicus lifted the plating in his gauntleted hand. "Sire. We found the remains of a great beast made of metals and wires, we do not know its origins, but my men are stripping it down as we speak and preparing the remains for transport to you by two carts," he explained to the smoke cloud, Garrick Thain's visage scrutinizing.

"How impressive, Captain. Were you able to ascertain its death?" The King of Kurn asked curiously, to which Grehner shook his bearded head.

"No, My King. My men were searching the tunnels for signs of the intruders when some came across the creature. Its scales are light as wood, but sturdy and smooth like metal. I thought it best to collect it for your interest."

"I see," replied Thain. "You've done well. I eagerly await this puzzle's arrival; it may prove very useful to me. What of the intruders? Have you located them yet?"

Atolicus grit his teeth, lips thinning in frustration before he uttered a curt word. "No." His eyes flashed angrily. "But we will find them, Your Majesty. They cannot be far beyond our grasp; I swear to you." The captain said firmly, attempting to ingratiate himself to the king out of survival instinct alone. Garrick Thain seemed unconcerned.

"Of course, Captain. Of course," Thain said smoothly. "And if there are more of these creatures in the caverns, I want one alive to study," he added.

Atolicus Grehner nodded quickly, eager to please his master. "As you desire, My King." he said, bowing his head. "With the added troops I've requested, we will search the caves quickly. There is nowhere for the invaders to hide."

"Mm." Garrick Thain replied without commitment, waving the smoke cloud to disperse without further command. Grehner stood there, watching the cloud float away with squinted eyes. He turned, carrying the large scale in his hand as he stormed through the tunnels and only paused to grab the first soldier he saw.

"You there. Find me a tradesman among the soldiers. Now." Atolicus commanded, the soldier gave a quick salute then lowered his hand and leaned forward.

"Well, I'm a tradesman, Sir. One of the mine's metalworkers, just like m'father was," the soldier said.

Grehner grinned darkly, thrusting the white scale against the soldier's chest plate with a resounding bang. "Good. Attach a handle and strap to this. I want it as a functional shield by morning."

The soldier twitched, almost stumbling back when the scale plate struck his chest. "Oof. Y-Yes, sir! But I'm supposed to be backing up Plasse, sir. He's back there, going through the caverns. You said two-man teams, sir." The soldier explained, hugging the plate to his chest and looking quite confused as to which order took precedence.

The Captain growled. "Then return to the camp and send another man in your place, IDIOT!" He roared the word, which made the soldier jump and run as fast as he could in his plate armor down the tunnel.

"Yes, sir! Sorry, sir!" The frightened trooper called out as he fled his commander's anger and left Atolicus seething in the tunnel. The man cracked his neck with a sharp, stiff turn of his head and proceeded to follow the frightened soldier's path toward camp.

Standing around was never Atolicus Grehner's strong point. He liked to keep busy. Even when he was overseeing the mines, he could engage in amusing torment of the miners and their families to keep himself occupied but here in the caves with nothing but his own men hard at work; the captain was growing bored. He swept into his lavish, large tent on the wide chasm floor near the white worm's corpse and sat down on his bed cot to consider his options.

His tent was well decorated as he expected of his men, each of his required furnishings was available from the wooden desk that he preferred to sit at when filling out his paperwork to his favorite potted Ficus plant beside it. The rack where his armor would be stored while he slept was near the far wall opposite his coat and his favored crimson and black standard rug was unrolled on the floor. All was as he required it to be.

While he was thinking, a voice called from beyond the tent. "Permission to enter, Sir!" The voice asked, prompting Atolicus to stand and reply. "Granted." A soldier swept through the tent flaps with a metal plate carrying dried meat, a triangle of cheese, a torn hunk of bread and one vine of purple grapes on it.

"Meal, sir. Forgive the intrusion," the soldier said, moving swiftly to set the plate on the desk and exit just as fast. Atolicus did not thank the man, instead moving to sit down in the wooden chair that accompanied his desk to eat.

A few minutes later, another soldier swept through the flaps without asking. "Report from the search, sir." The trooper announced, standing at attention while Grehner scowled at him and chewed a bit of cheese. The captain grunted, nodding, but the man just stood there like a statue.

After a few moments of awkward silence, Atolicus swallowed cheese and snarled. "Speak, fool. Speak!"

The trooper jerked defensively at the snarl. "W-we finished searching the tunnels, no sign of the invaders. The men report three small nests of Gnolls, all cleared out. The only region we've not yet searched is up the chasm, sir!" He spoke quickly, trying to control the fear in his tone as he relayed his summary.

Grehner snorted. "Take four men up the ledge then," he said, which the soldier replied to with a firm salute of thumping the chest plate of his arm with a gauntleted fist.

"Now, sir?" The soldier asked to confirm.

"YES NOW!" roared Atolicus, slamming his own fist on the desktop with a resounding thump that made every soldier outside the tent jump.

"Yes, sir!" The reporting soldier said, all but running out of the tent as fast as his metal plated boots could carry him. Atolicus raged inside. His men were idiots and he had nothing to do but wait, wait, wait. If only they had found the invaders, he could occupy himself with torturing them one by one just for the pleasure of it. He would rip out their fingernails, cut off their toes, bounce their skulls off the rock wall over and over and over again.

That little psychopathic daydream only settled the man for a brief time, long enough to finish eating his food and chuckle to himself. Unfortunately, reality set in and left the captain frustrated again as he stood up and walked through the tent flap to find only black armored soldiers milling around. They were taking a meal, the white worm nearly fully stripped into piles of like materials save for the massive, glassy eye at its head. Atolicus stared into the eye, wondering over its purpose.

"When the carts arrive, I want the eye and body on one and the piles on another taken directly to the capital. Only two men per cart, sleeping in shifts. Unload and return here immediately," he commanded openly to an instant call of "Yes, Sir" in unison.

Atolicus walked slowly across the stone floor toward the eye, crouching down to look at it more closely. Huge, round, but when touched, it was glass. He pulled his gauntlet off and ran his bare hand down the smooth contour of the glass eye, marveling at its design. He was just coming to some profound conclusion about the object when a soldier came running down the ledge and interrupted the thought.

"Sir!"

Whatever sudden insight Grehner had nearly come to was lost to a scowl. "What?!" he snapped.

"There's an exit high up at the top of this ledge, it winds around the chasm all the way up."

The Captain growled, standing up. He stalked up the ledge and around for as long as it took, growling and grumbling to himself as time wore on. Near the height of the cave structure, one of the four men he'd sent up ahead waited.

"Sir. You're not going to believe this," the scout said eagerly, excitement in his voice.

"Stand aside!" Atolicus snarled, storming past the man toward the lighted portal out of the mountain. He marched through, finding the other two scouts looking over the edge of the landing outside.

Atolicus Grehner marched slowly to the ledge between his men, looking out over the vast expanse of spires, towers, and rooftops. His dark eyes squinted in the fading daylight, trying to make sense of what lay before his very eyes. The captain rummaged into his belt, finding a fresh, black candle which he lit with a tinderstick and tossed onto the rocky floor but despite the thick, acrid smoke that billowed from the burning wax; it did not coalesce into the visage of Garrick Thain.

Grehner growled. "You, stay here. Shift change in five hours. None are permitted to pass between save Black Vanguard soldiers," he commanded, the scouts replying immediately that they understood.

Back down the spiraling ledge, The Captain marched hurriedly. Eager to report to his master, eager to do something more than these mundanities. He could not wait for orders to take the discovered city, to reap what treasures might be found within its walls for the glory of the Black Vanguard, for Kurn, but most importantly, for himself. Atolicus Grehner looked forward to the war that was sure to come. A dark, pleased smile settled on his bearded face, one that unsettled his men as he reached the chasm floor and passed them by into the torchlit tunnels. The Battle for Solaria would not be long coming and soon, the Black Vanguard would be unstoppable.

Chapter Twenty:
Epilogue?

It took the construct called Sixer a full hour to attach himself to the rejuvenator, shifting his chest plate aside so he could wire the machine into his personal power crystal located underneath the orb that was his central core processing unit. Sixer reasoned that there was enough solar energy in the redundancy cells of the rejuvenator that he would only need to start the device.

His metal hand outstretched, pressing the green power button. His core crystal dimmed, the blue lights in his head sphere simultaneously began to darken as the rejuvenator took the energy and spooled up with a whirring sound. Lights and screens on the control panel winked on, displaying the image of an apple before gauges of energy levels appeared. Sixer remained still, letting the machine feed off of his crystal until one of the screen's showed a one percent charge on its display then the construct disconnected the line.

He reattached it to the power conduit, his movements slow, sluggish as his crystal core was partially drained of what power it had left. Sixer stood, staring at the charge display while it slowly ticked numbers up from one percent to two, two percent to three and onwards. It took nearly another hour for the crystal to charge with solar power and when the machine chimed that the charge was complete, Sixer took the crystal from the mooring plate inside the rejuvenator then carried it over to the power generator.

The instant that the crystal was affixed in the housing, slid into place like a giant fuse in a fuse box; the generator whirred alive. Sixer closed the glass encasement shield while the generator began to glow a brilliant, empowered blue that moved like air traffic lights in a row down the sides of the colossal casing. The faster the procession of lights cycled; the more power was flowing from it. Sixer looked upon this and saw it was good, operating at maximum efficacy.

Satisfied with his work performance, the construct moved away from the generator to begin to turn on all of the city's functional control systems with flicks of toggles and presses of small green buttons. Water pumps began to thrum beneath the roads, lights in every tower, spire, street and room began to glow gently. Finally, the drone battery chamber was turned on and a crystal core was placed inside its containment shield housing before Sixer stopped moving altogether. He stood perfectly still, almost dormant, save for those two blue lights emanating from the metal sphere that was his head. Work complete, standing by for replacement core.

The lights caught Leeni, Yoder, and The Wizard by surprise. Yoder drew his sword at first, preparing to defend himself until The Wizard cheered with a laugh. "Hahah! Huzzah, it looks like your robot got the city running again!"

Yoder slid his sword away with a look of relieved comfort. "Good job, Sixer," he said to himself more than anyone else, grateful for the good news. Soon, they would take care of poor Perrixstar.

"Yoder?"

He heard Leeni call his name questioningly, turning around. He found the girl standing in the round doorway of the first house by the gateway they'd entered from with a most confused and alarmed expression on her face. "What is it?" He asked. "What's wrong?" A chill ran up his spine, were they too late to save his friend?

"Come, you've got to see this…" Leeni said, beckoning with a wave.

As Yoder and The Wizard crossed through the round portal inside the building, both noted someone talking. Leeni was the one who pointed the person out, but it wasn't a person at all.

"...to evacuate the city by airship. You have three hours to proceed to the transportation depot and board our flagship, The Inevitable. Thank you and God bless." A woman's voice was saying from the glass pane mounted on the wall, what you would call a television. It was a woman, gray of hair and very fine featured that stared back at them. Yoder even thought she was pretty if a bit old.

The woman's visage twitched, and she began to speak again. "Citizens of Solari Prime. Due to the fall of Levistrax, our land is now uninhabitable, and we are cut off from the outside world save for air travel. As such, all citizens have been ordered to take their essential belongings and are to evacuate the city by airship. You have three hours to proceed to the transportation depot and board our flagship, The Inevitable. Thank you and God bless."

"Huh," said Yoder.

The Tales of Halziyon

Book 2: City of Eld - Yoder and his friends stumbled upon the fabled City of Eld, Solaria, beyond the Razor's Teeth while seeking to save Halziyon. Now, the adventurers must search through the city for a way to save their gravely injured friend with the Black Vanguard snapping at their heels. Can Yoder find a way to keep Solaria from falling into the clutches of Garrick Thain, Mage-King of Kurn? What marvels lay in the silent, lost city of magic and science beyond compare?

Book 3: The Hero's Flaw - The explosive conclusion of Tales of Halziyon is here. Yoder's friends rally amidst a war between the Mirrored Circle of Halziyon and Kurn's mad king, Garrick Thain. While Leeni Vex aids the Army of Magic, The Wizard leads a small force through Kurn to stop Thain's war machine before its activation. The fate of Halziyon rests in the hands of Yoder's companions, but where is the Hero?

More Books by the Author

Jisedai - Gabriel is a killer for the mega-corporation that raised him, trained in the ancient arts of Bushido.

Hana was kidnapped, forced into a world of depravity and darkness.

When the two meet by chance on the grimy, rain-soaked streets of a frightening future Harajuku sector, it changes both their lives forever. For honor, Gabriel must now face the group of trained killers and soldiers that he swore loyalty to and bloody his white hare katana to protect the young girl and her strange pet.

Dark Angels and wicked assassins wage war in the ruins beyond the borders of oppressed Tokyo in Jisedai!

Legacy of Heroes - Ten years after the death of Paragon: The World's Greatest Superhero, heroism has withered in the city.

A hidden threat keeps superhumans in hiding until a teenage boy dons the red, white, and blue of Paragon once more and sets off a chain reaction that exposes the truth behind the hero's death and what preys on new superhumans in the shadows.

Join Dasani Watson as he brings hope back to the city. Meet James, afraid of his own dark power, and Amy, a girl with devastating powers who wants to fit in somewhere. Together, they'll battle villains new and old and take on this Legacy of Heroes.

www.ingramcontent.com/pod-product-compliance
Lightning Source LLC
LaVergne TN
LVHW091546060526
838200LV00036B/723